MOVE OVER, MINERVA

Thea Allen

This is a work of fiction. Any references to historical events, real people or real places are used fictitiously. Other names, characters, places and events are the products of the author's imagination, and any resemblance to actual persons living or dead, events or locales is entirely coincidental.

Copyright © 2025 by Thea Allen.

All rights reserved. With the exception of the translated text of the curse upon the thief of Vilbia and the dedication of the divinities of the Emperors and Mars Camulus, no part of this book may be reproduced or used in any manner without written permission of the copyright owner except for use of quotations in a book review.

First paperback edition April 2025.

Cover design, book design and map by Creative Tributaries. Fonts used under OpenFont or Creative Commons licenses and include *Mr.B* by Etherbrian, *Vollkorn* by Friedrich Althausen, *EB Garamond* by Georg Duffner and Octavio Pardo, and *Baskervville* by ANRT.

The translated curse upon the thief of Vilbia and the dedication to the divinities of the Emperors and Mars Camulus are adapted within the dialogue of the characters. The curse is provided verbatim from the Roman Inscriptions of Britain translation within the Author's Note (RIB 154 and RIB 3014, https://romaninscriptionsofbritain.org, accessed 8 June 2024). The translations are used within this book under a Creative Commons 4.0 license (https://creativecommons.org/licenses/by/4.0).

NO AI TRAINING: Without in any way limiting the author's [and publisher's] exclusive rights under copyright, any use of this publication to "train" generative artificial intelligence (AI) technologies to generate text is expressly prohibited. The author reserves all rights to license uses of this work for generative AI training and development of machine learning language models.

ISBN 978-1-7637664-0-2 (paperback)
ISBN 978-1-7637664-1-9 (ebook)

BISG Classifications:
FIC022060 (FICTION/Mystery & Detective/Historical)
FIC014010 (FICTION/Historical/Ancient)
FIC022100 (FICTION/Mystery & Detective/Amateur Sleuth)

Published by Creative Tributaries
www.creativetributaries.com

A catalogue record for this book is available from the National Library of Australia

MOVE OVER, MINERVA

A Laelius Calvus Mystery
Book 1

Thea Allen

For Todd, Emma and Megan
for putting up with my strange ideas.

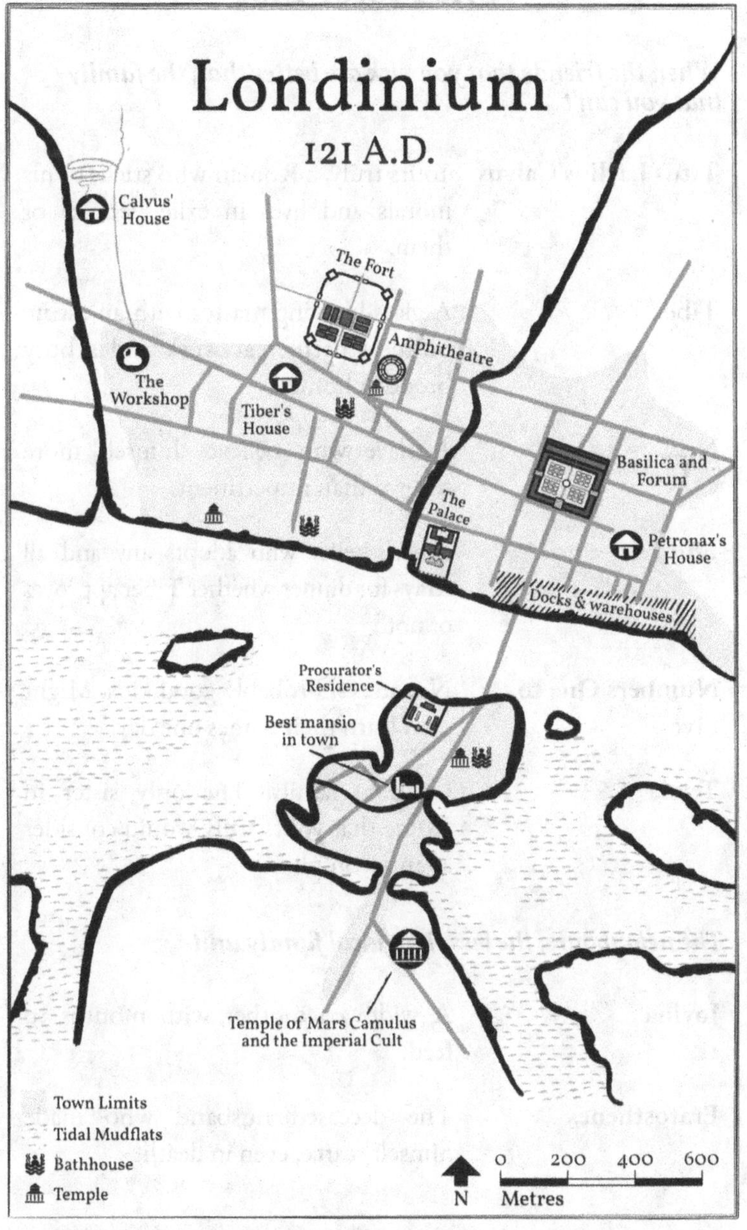

Londinium
121 A.D.
Calvus' House
The Fort
Amphitheatre
The Workshop
Tiber's House
Basilica and Forum
The Palace
Petronax's House
Docks & warehouses
Procurator's Residence
Best mansio in town
Temple of Mars Camulus and the Imperial Cult
Town Limits
Tidal Mudflats
Bathhouse
Temple
N
Metres
0   200   400   600

Character List

When the friends that you pick are better than the family that you can't

Titus Laelius Calvus Yours truly, a Roman who sticks to his morals and lives in exile because of them.

Tiber A glass-blowing master with an astute business partner at work and a busy brood at home.

Nux A slave who believes himself more shrewd than impertinent.

Enica Tiber's wife, who adopts any and all strays for dinner whether Tiber approves or not.

Numbers One to Five Not strays. Probably good kids. Might even learn their names one day.

Tertia Genuine family. The only sister in Rome that yours truly would consider as an accomplice.

The neighbours; the less than ideal family unit

Jovina A widowed mother with mouths to feed.

Eratosthenes The deceased husband who made himself scarce, even in death.

Pacatus

The dour son of Jovina's first husband, down two fathers now.

The twins

Jovina and Eratosthenes' twin babes, who eat things they really shouldn't.

The devout ideal

Memor

A temple haruspex, just as at home when elbows-deep in entrails as he is in a good, hot bath.

Marcella

His niece, who disappears off to the shops whenever possible.

Vilbia

His other niece, who just disappears.

The singles

Petronax

A most clumsy priest.

Augustalis

A slighted lover.

Varro-with-the-gimpy-leg

An ex-legionary with a bone to pick with the gods. A leg bone, probably.

Cocceius Nonnus

A quarry foreman who just wants his bills paid.

Amatus

A stressed-out resident of Aquae Sulis.

A Language Lesson

Amphora
A ceramic vessel that can range in size from a table-top jug to one half the height of a human, and usually filled with deliciousness - wine, olive oil, a sauce made from fish that's been left to ferment in the sun for a month, and so forth.

Augury and Augurs
The art of interpreting omens sent by the gods, and the men who profess the ability to do so.

Cullet
Broken glass shards to be melted down and recycled, obtained by dropping your wine glass onto the mosaic floor and then instructing the slaves to sweep it up.

Echidna
A horrific snake monster of ancient Greek origin with suspiciously feminine attributes.

Frigidarium
The coldest pool in the bathhouse, a plunge bath for those with a masochistic take on getting clean.

Hades;
Tartarus;
Fields of Elysium;
Asphodel Meadows
The underworld within which one would spend one's afterlife; the section with fire and sharp sticks; the section with flowers, singing and dancing; and the bureaucratic housing estate for those who deserve neither torment nor bliss.

Harpy	A horrific bird monster of ancient Greek origin with suspiciously feminine attributes.
Haruspex	An official diviner who examines sacrificial animal guts to interpret the gods' rather obtuse method of delivering messages to us mere mortals. Writing letters would just be too easy and no fun at all.
Mansio	A guest-house of superior quality, where the drinking vessels are made of glass and they don't expect the patrons to steal the bed linen.
Medusa	Another horrific snake monster of ancient Greek origin with suspiciously feminine attributes. The old story tellers didn't seem to like powerful women.
Oceanid	Any one of the three thousand daughters of the Titans Oceanus and Tethys. Their parents probably didn't remember all their names. Or birthdays.
Saturnalia	That festive time at the end of the year where gifts are given, too much food is eaten, candles are lit and drunk uncles tell cringey stories.

Taverna   A drinking establishment where the drinking vessels are made of wood or cheap ceramic and they expect the clientele to steal anything not nailed down.

Tepidarium   A much more pleasant warm bath, one in which a sensible bather would want to linger.

Typhon   Yet another horrific snake monster, but one that goes against the grain – this time with suspiciously masculine attributes. Not all monsters are women, it seems.

Londinium

121 A.D.

1

I'm going to start my own religion.

I've given it a lot of thought. It's going to have funny hats, routine animal sacrifice, and treasuries. Especially treasuries. Money can't be burned and eaten, so what else can the priests do but to spend it on the gods' behalf on useful things, like comfortable beds?

Oh, and priests named 'Petronax' will be banned. I know a priest named 'Petronax', and he's an idiot.

My sentiment towards Petronax was confirmed as I stood at the open graveside of my neighbour, watching his widow as she stood over the open bier of not-my-neighbour, screeching 'I want my money back' into Petronax's face. I had had my doubts that the late Flavius Eratosthenes would be greatly missed but this wasn't quite what I had imagined.

For starters, no-one should have noticed that the body of Eratosthenes was missing at all. When his widow Jovina stopped the proceedings, muttered 'the lying bastard thinks he can take it with him', then pulled out a knife and with surprising deftness cut into the shroud to reclaim the one signet ring worth any cash, it was not the slender, olive hand of a clerk with Egyptian heritage that emerged. This was the hand of an older, more muscular Gaul.

Secondly, all of this should have caused a greater stir among the mourners. Gathered together were Eratosthenes' twin babes (who were too young to know what was going on as they sat devouring a repast of twigs and stones), Jovina's twelve-year-old son (from her first, equally-as-missed, husband), a handful of mourners contractually obliged to be there, and myself, who had only attended to avoid the inevitable harassment that I would have received from Jovina had I failed to show up. Aside from Jovina's reaction, all that this farce had managed to cause was a raised eyebrow or two.

Three at the most.

For the moment, Jovina had paused to draw breath and the eyes of the mourners fell to me. I sighed and stepped towards her. It seemed I had lost a vote I didn't even know was taking place.

"Perhaps a runner could be sent. Pac, for example..." I said, glancing at her eldest. Pacatus stared back at me with baleful eyes.

"Piss off, Calvus." Jovina was not impressed. Thank goodness. I nodded once and turned to leave. "Where are you going?"

"Pissing off, as instructed."

"No, you're not. We're all going to sit here until this, this... imbecile finds my husband."

Perhaps all of this was to be expected. Eratosthenes could bore even the staunchest of listeners to tears. It was fitting that his funeral should be spent with us all perched on rocks within the cemetery with our eyes glazed over.

I had thought him an unusual choice of husband for Jovina, until I had realised that it was all the result of a misunderstanding. Being an imperial freedman with a suitably stable desk job in the palace of Britannia's Proconsul implied a steady income.

He was not that good at his job. As a slave, I think he had been awarded his freedom just to get rid of him when no buyer could be duped. Even that plan had not gone well – as a freedman, Eratosthenes had fallen under the patronage of the Palace and its officials were obliged to see him secure. He turned down their offers of bucolic bliss, far from the hustle of Londinium's inner workings, and opted to stay exactly where he was, working the job he loved with the people who did not love him in return.

He plodded on; they gave him subtle messages to leave by frequently forgetting to include him in the pay run.

As Petronax floundered, waving his arms at the bier-carriers as they disappeared around the bend and back to town, Jovina flopped down beside me. Her babies were making good their escape, dragging themselves along on their stomachs to disappear between the marble crypts. She didn't seem to notice so Pacatus dragged his heels after them to round them up. The other mourners feigned interest in the nearby inscriptions and generally avoided eye contact.

"Why do you use him?" I asked, nodding in the direction Petronax had gone.

"He's the only one offering the service," she replied.

"The Vejovis and Libitina Funeral Club?"

"That's the one."

"I'm pretty sure he pockets every spare coin he gets from that."

"Oh, I forgot. The rich boy here can afford better."

She was probably right. If my time ended prematurely, my father would gleefully pay for a full service. Light the fires himself, probably. However, Eratosthenes and Jovina did not have relatives honing their fire-starters, so they were members of Petronax's funeral club, the Funeral Club of Vejovis and Libitina. They paid their monthly dues and in return the club would cover their funeral expenses and provide them with occasional dinners with the other members.

I often wondered what they talked about at their social dinners. What a bleak, regular reminder of their inevitable demise, meeting with those whose only interest in you was to hope that you died first so that they could see the quality of the service.

In fact, Petronax ran two funeral clubs. The Funeral Club of the Triple Coventina catered for Celtic patrons. It had middling success, but Petronax remained hopeful. This was no doubt the source of the confusion that day, when a member of each had died at the same time. The biers that Petronax had sent to collect the remains had become jumbled somewhere along the way. Someone probably should have noticed that, too.

"So, the cheap bastard won't even fork out for cremation?" I asked. Jovina snorted.

"Nowhere in the constitution does it say how he's going to dispose of us. Still," her brow creased as she cast her eye over the open pit, "it's better than being tossed in the river, I guess."

"If they can find him. Not that that has ever mattered, I haven't seen him in months. The well-toned Augustalis, however—"

"Oh, piss off, Calvus."

"Really?"

"Yes, I don't want you here." I rose to leave. "And on your way home, pick me up some bread. I've got mouths to feed, you know."

I rolled my eyes and left.

2

You know what else my religion will need? Ornate glass offering vessels. Expensive ones.

I didn't go home after leaving the funeral. Nor did I go to the baker as Jovina had hoped. I went to visit my pet project: a glass-blower's workshop a few streets from the fort. My business partner, Tiber, would hate to hear our workshop described so blithely – he's trying to make an honest living feberom the place. He also hates being called 'Tiber.' He doesn't get his way about a lot of things.

"I've never been there, there's no use naming me for the bloody thing" – is his usual argument. "Might as well call me Britannicus, or Tamesis. At least I can get my feet wet in that one."

He tried to hit me with a blow pipe the day that I voiced my opinion that he should mimic the Romans. Conquer Britannia, I suggested, or at least the banks of the Tamesis, and then he could give himself a geographic name, like Scipio Africanus. After all, his father had been a resettled Roman soldier, from whom he had inherited his actual name of 'Gaius Barbatius Tiberinus' in the first place, so conquest was in his blood.

Besides, I thought that the name 'Tiber Tamesis' was alluring in its alliteration.

The one flaw to my moniker-making plan was that his mother was of the Trinovantes tribe, traditionally living north of Londinium itself. Tiber was fiercely proud of his Celtic heritage, despite having chosen to make his living mastering a craft that came from the opposite side of the Roman Empire. His Celtic ancestors had tended to be just as warlike as the Romans, but were much less likely to adopt a Roman nickname afterwards.

In any case, life in Londinium had settled down into a rhythm of commerce and imported creature comforts, and few had any wish to return to the conflict that would see the city burned to the ground.

Again.

I was surprised to find Tiber manning the shop as I walked through the front door. He sat perched on a stool in the corner, his robust form at odds with the delicate rainbow on display before him. He was a brilliant worker of glass but the least natural salesman I've ever seen, resorting to technical discussion of cullet quality or the exact proportion of colourant needed to bring out the reds and blues and overcome the natural yellow-brown tint of the finished product.

We tried to keep him out of the shop front if at all possible.

"Where's Nux?" I asked by way of greeting.

Tiber nodded his head towards the workshop in the back.

"The boy's resting up for tonight. You're back early."

"Eratosthenes was late for his own funeral and Jovina kicked me out. What's happening tonight?"

He blinked but said nothing of my report. Tackling my second sentence would be less likely to induce a headache.

"It's a workday tomorrow, he's got a furnace to bring up to temperature." I winced. By 'bring up to temperature', Tiber meant that someone had to sit up overnight putting new wood on the fire.

Every seven minutes.

For twelve hours.

I feigned interest in a set of red mould-blown cups on the shelf next to me. I didn't remember them; Tiber must have made them with Nux's assistance.

Nux was Tiber's one and only slave. I say 'one-and-only', but it's still one more than I had. Tiber called him 'the boy' but in reality Nux was less than a year younger than me and had spent much longer learning the craft.

And he was far more imaginative than his master. His sales spiel included talk of skilled boutique artisans coaxing individual works of art into existence in aqua, amber, rose-red and the purple of Emperors. That's why he normally covered the shop unless there was a truly awful task that no free person would volunteer to do, like bringing the furnace up to temperature.

Tiber's already-wrinkled brow furrowed even more.

"You're meant to be helping me tomorrow, remember?"

Ah Hades.

"Oh?" I replied. "You know, I really must go check on..." I had a thoroughly believable coughing fit as I pushed through the rear door into the workshop.

"Calvus, you will be here, right? Locinna's order needs finishing, it's going to be late—" With a tug, the door swung shut behind me but it wasn't enough to drown out the expletive that followed my departure.

Glass is such a crisp, clean product but the workshop that produced it wasn't. The square room behind the shop we used mostly as storage. Tools on the left, finished works on the right, crates of unworked glass and broken shards for recycling, called 'cullet', in the middle. We didn't make the glass from scratch here – no-one in Londinium was stupid enough to put themselves through that. Instead, we had a reliable supplier who brought over cullet from the mainland, ready to be crafted.

And 'craft' it we could do with ease. We only had the furnace capacity for two glassworkers to be on the go at the same time, but that didn't stop Tiber from stocking up on every shaped tweezer, cutter, tong and paddle imaginable. Beyond the shelves piled high with tools, organised and catalogued in some system that made sense only to Tiber, the back door led into the semi-walled yard in which the round furnace had been built, near a cooling oven of similar size.

Nux lay on his pallet wedged in between shelves of pincers and the blowpipe stand. I wasn't sure if he was still awake when I entered or if my escape from Tiber woke him, but he opened one eye as I crept past.

"He's starting to think he's got the bad end of this deal, Calvus."

"You keep out of it."

"I'd love to, but I'm the one who has to pick up the slack."

I put on my best affronted citizen face and looked him over. "You'd better watch it, boy, or I'll report the impertinence you show to your master's business partner to the man himself."

"Apprentice. The impertinence I show to his apprentice."

"Partner. I own this place."

"Apprentice. You own the building, not the business."

"Shut up."

The corners of his mouth curled upwards in victory as he rolled to face away from me. He was wrong, I was definitely Tiber's partner. I owned the building to be sure, and graciously allowed Tiber to occupy it rent free in return for teaching me the craft. I wasn't paid for my efforts in the workshop, as an apprentice would; I received a share of the sales from the shop. Therefore, I shared the risk.

Therefore, definitely a partner, not an apprentice. I made sure to knock over the blow pipe stand as I pushed on through to the yard and made good my escape over the back wall.

***

You might be thinking by now that I spend my life trying to avoid contact with all other human beings. You'd probably be right, but I bought Jovina a loaf of bread on the way home. I'm not a complete monster.

Despite its remote location, Londinium reminds me of home. A mini-Rome-away-from-Rome, a place of perpetual scaffolding as building strains to keep pace with demand. It has mansions and slums, interspersed with temples and baths, a forum, a palace, a fort and an amphitheatre. Graffiti was appearing that advertised the impending arrival of the 'Tarraconensis Troupe' – travelling Hispanic acrobats and dancers – and one could buy papyrus grown on the banks of the Nile at Alexandria. Everyone is jostled in together in a burgeoning city; there are well over forty thousand citizens and slaves, freedmen and provincials, soldiers, merchants, craftsmen and bureaucrats from across the Empire. It is the Roman Empire rebuilt in city-form.

Until you get out to where I live.

I squelched my way down the side of a small, forested ridge with the loaf tucked under my arm. Any further northwest from town and our houses would have encroached on brickearth quarries and cemeteries. The narrow river flat to which I was destined was otherwise inaccessible and had been deemed unsuitable for any industry, so a few families had adopted it as home, each with their own motives for wanting peace, quiet and concealment.

Eratosthenes had claimed the more desirable of our two dwellings for his family. Built upon a slight rise, theirs was up out of the marsh and safe from seasonal fluctuations in water level. They had three rooms of luxury, a fenced yard with two hens, and a small outbuilding containing the tools Eratosthenes had purchased for his intended vegetable garden.

He never broke ground on his plan, but that had nothing to do with his untimely demise. Apparently, he had bought his tools two years before he had even met Jovina.

I pushed through the gate and rattled the front door of the house. Jovina had had the wits to latch the lock before embarking on the funeral procession. The front step was dry and sheltered by the overhang of a thatched roof. I considered abandoning the bread on the step but the hens, Coquam and Pluma, were already scratching their way closer with evil intent.

Especially Coquam. Her red feathers were sleek and pristine compared to the smaller, oft-harassed Pluma. Coquam was capable of atrocities beyond the intelligence of your average chicken. Her reign of terror was something I would not tolerate, and I did as any noble Roman had done before me when faced with tyranny and oppression. As I turned to leave, and her beady eye met mine, I showed her who was boss. I tried to land my boot on her.

I missed, but I'm sure it was a lesson well learned.

As the person with the dubious honour of owning the last house on this particular track, the path to my dwelling rapidly dwindled, worn into the grass by the tread of my own sandals. A rocky outcrop shaded by a massive walnut tree separated our properties and as I squeezed between the boulders, I stopped short upon seeing a most unwelcome sight.

No matter what my intentions, everyone ends up wanting my blood in some form or another. This is why I try to avoid contact with all other human beings. So, my heart dropped upon spying a legionary from the nearby fort waiting on my doorstep. He was a big man and he did not look pleased.

"Titus Laelius Calvus?"

"I'm looking for him too, friend. You wait your turn. What do you want him for?"

His lip curled and he reached into a satchel at his side. I braced as he pulled his arm out but his fingers were wrapped around nothing more substantial than a thick roll of papyrus.

"I'm not a private messenger," the man said as he thrust it into my hands and pushed past me, his boots slipping in a somewhat undignified manner.

I'm an educated man. I know that words can be more dangerous than any blade, so it was with some trepidation that I took the roll inside. Don't be mistaken by the crummy façade of my house. Whoever built this place had looked around at the available land, identified the place in which the most water accumulated after rain before draining down to the creek, and had taken it upon themselves to build a two-room abode in that very spot.

But I was a man with connections. Honest. I had chosen to buy here; I wasn't forced into it.

Well maybe I was a little forced into it – it was what I could afford after I had spent a bunch of money on the workshop.

But the point is, that letter could have been from anyone – the best lawyers in Rome, some horrid informer paid to track me down, anyone. I took it inside, dropped Jovina's bread on the rough-hewn slab on bricks that passed for a dining table, and examined the seal. I didn't recognise it, so I had no excuse not to break it open.

My hands trembled slightly as the pages unfurled, revealing light, loopy handwriting...

Oh.

It was just from my little sister.

Laelia Tertia to her dear brother Titus Laelius Calvus

Surprise!

We gave instructions for this to be delivered to the most pathetic man in the Empire, and low and behold now you are reading these words.

Funny. Tertia thought herself very funny.

But she was not as clever as she thought. A year ago, on the night I fled Rome, she was the only person to whom I told of my intentions. She knew where I was. The mystery as to how she managed to get a personal letter delivered by the military and not at the astronomical expense of a private courier was also soon answered:

I'm writing to inform you that we are not all the cause of our father's future apoplexy. I've changed my mind about joining you. I admit, I had been tempted to that night and numerous since, but then I met Marcus. Or rather, then Father introduced me to Marcus and it turns out that sometimes his schemes actually lead to quite pleasing results.

Marcus Caelius Pollio, the soon-to-be sire of your future nieces and nephews. Father has brokered the deal of his dreams in this marriage – a Caelius no less, a holder of the office of tribune and divinely favoured by manner of his birth as the twin of a Praetorian.

And not just any Praetorian, but one on the staff of Septicius Clarus, and you know what that means. I'll be the wife of the brother of the assistant of the Prefect who advises Emperor Hadrian himself! Father is over the moon!

I needed a drink.

I had a small bench in the corner that served as my kitchen with, optimistically, two plates and two bowls. No-one had ever come to dinner, but I lived in hope. Something else it contained was a massive selection of misshapen drinking glasses; all serviceable, all unsellable but rescued from the workshop cullet pile none-the-less. There were about twenty in all, rejects that Tiber and I had produced.

Well, only one was Tiber's. It owed its existence to the fact that I had bumped him as he was placing it in the cooling oven.

I selected a robust beaker and filled it with a dark brew of pure nectar, although this nectar had its origins among rougher gods than those at home and was not typically partaken amid marble and tyrian purple. 'True' Romans, the ones that felt the need to write about how perfectly Roman they were in copious volumes, looked down upon beer but in reality it was just as vital a drink in the provinces as wine was within cities and luxurious country villas.

It gave me the courage to continue.

You would like the two brothers – behind their tough professional exteriors lies the humorous, thoughtful interiors of two men who really don't see the point of grandeur and glory. Marcus even does the truly radical at times, using his position of Tribune of the Plebs to actually try to help fellow Plebs in need. Father hasn't seen that contradictory side of their personalities yet. That is just as well, for the benefits that it brings you, even in exile. Use of the military post, for example?

No doubt this letter was delivered by some disgruntled soldier, put out by the fact he has to search for you because some pompous officer in Rome had the generosity to let his future sister-in-law stay in touch with her disgraced brother. To that end, I have enclosed some blank papyrus and official instructions to include your reply within the local garrison's own outgoings. That's if you have the audacity to approach the fort.

Father won't send his regards. To be fair, he doesn't know that I'm writing this, but even so.

What were you thinking? To say Father is displeased is an understatement, or at least a disservice to all the slightly peeved people in the world. He can't disinherit you, that would return the Laelius Calvii to the backwater of society. He can't disown you – the only son in a gaggle of daughters? You are the only hope of his name continuing in future generations.

So, he's come up with a plan. He pretends that time stopped the day you departed, and it will restart the moment you walk back in the door espousing the error of your ways. Until then, no mention is to be made of you. Laelius Calvus Senior attends to his girls and that's that.

But I don't believe that for a moment. He's looking for you. Stay safe. Tell no-one, trust no-one, be the master of disguise, the man without a name, an enigma, a mystery, a riddle. Just don't be yourself...

3

"So, marry Jovina," Tiber said in response to my full, detailed account of the contents of the letter.

He had calmed down considerably when I turned up for work the next morning. The furnace and cooling ovens were ready and Nux had passed into a grateful sleep back on his pallet. "That'll solve two problems," Tiber continued, "your wilfulness and Jovina's need of support to raise her orphans."

"I'm not going to marry Jovina."

"Whatever. Got that ready?" Tiber nodded at the mould in my hands. It had been a long day and I was dawdling more than he would have liked.

There are few professions where I would ensure that the professional in question had steady hands. The first, being my barber, for obvious reasons with a blade against my throat. The second, gods forbid I should ever need one, being a surgeon, for reasons likewise. The third was a glass-blower while he was holding a luminscently-hot bulb of molten glass at the end of a blowpipe, as he lowered it into the narrow hole of a soot-lined ceramic mould, a hairsbreadth from where my fingers gripped the handles.

Within moments of his injury-defying move, Tiber had blown the glass to fill the mould and waited as I gently shook the mould free. I clamped a different pole to the bottom of the bottle to hold it, detached the blow pipe, and Tiber thrust the glass back into the furnace to reheat. Once ready, he sat spinning the pole along a board strapped to his leg and smoothed out the shape of the neck, pinching, reheating and tweezering the thing into a narrow spout as it rapidly cooled. Glowing red gave way to a hint of its final pale green colour.

He swore as it failed to do his bidding.

"Bloody Dio, he's sold you old cullet. I knew I should have gone to see him myself."

The problem with making new glass vessels out of old broken cullet was that once it got too old, it became unworkable. Broken glass could be reused four, maybe five times, tops.

"You mentioned my name to him, right?" Tiber asked. "He keeps his best stuff for me."

"Don't remember, it probably came up." He glanced at me, clearly unimpressed. "Maybe he didn't have anything better. What are you going to do, make it from scratch?"

He didn't answer that and changed the subject, a move which worried me more than any voiced denial ever could. As he worked, I heated a new blob of glass destined to become the handles of the vessel.

"How is she going to manage now?" he asked, as a bleary-eyed Nux emerged into the lingering smoke to see what the fuss was about. He squatted in the corner of the yard and held his tongue.

"Jovina? Augustalis, I guess."

"Her lover?"

"He's 'round there whenever Eratosthenes isn't." I did a mental double-take and corrected myself. "Whenever Eratosthenes wasn't. Guess that's not a problem, now."

"A lover is a long way from financial security."

"You know I can't provide that yet."

"You can, you've just got to stop being such a spoiled brat and get to work around here."

"Spoiled brat? I am in exile, you know."

Tiber snorted. "My heart bleeds. Now, you've got four mould designs on the go, any one of which could be made up and sold if you'd just finish them off. Instead, you get them half done, get bored, then move onto the next idea. How much money have you got left in that strongbox of yours?"

My eyes narrowed. That strongbox was my safety plan in case I needed to return to Rome with my tail between my legs. Within it was just enough money for the return trip.

"She's not getting that."

Tiber looked at me and let the matter drop. With a bit more fussing about, I brought over my blob and touched it to the side of the bottle, stretching it out to form a handle. Tiber grabbed a wooden stick to pull it into a rounded shape, comfortable enough for a couple of fingers to grasp. "So, your father's on the warpath, huh?" he asked. "What happened? Got some rich aristocratic daughter knocked up?"

"Gods no. He'd love that. No, it's much worse. I've ruined the honour of his great-great-grandsons, yet unborn."

He looked me up and down, contemplating what preposterously anti-Roman thing I could have done to bring on my father's wrath.

"You ran naked through the heart of the Forum?"

I blinked. "What? No. What's going on in your mind to make it leap straight to that?"

He shrugged and gestured for me to open the door of the cooling oven. "Don't rightly care what you did, to be honest, as long as you don't muck things up for me here."

"You have no worries there." I looked around at the yard, bathed in orange, Tiber looking like a vitreous Vulcan in the sun's dying light, placing the last vessel of the day into the laden oven. "You and I are destined for great things. Wealth beyond our imagining."

"Well then, Croesus, to get wealth beyond your imagining you have to put in the work." He tossed me a broom. I started jabbing it at the floor in the hopes that Nux would be irritated by my clumsiness and take over. Never do a job well if you never want to do it again.

"I mean it, you know," I grumbled, my mood turning sour as Tiber scoffed at my ambition and Nux ignored my obvious hints with the broom. "The two of us shall facilitate the connection between the divine and mankind. Our glassware will glimmer with gifts, brim with benefactions, and carry the contributions of worship that will be brought forth by those prostrating themselves at our altar."

Tiber barked out a laugh. "What in Hades are you on about, Calvus?"

I struggled to get my thoughts in order, but Nux proved unexpectedly erudite from his wearily reflective position in the corner.

"He wants to start his own cult," he called out. I looked over to him in affirmation.

"Exactly. Everyone is seeking peace with the gods. We can help them. I want people to be excited about giving to the gods and it will be no less real than at any other temple."

Tiber, his expression unchanged, rubbed his brow. "Which god do you have in mind?"

"Dunno. Who's not worshipped here yet?" I leant on my broom and considered exotic gods with well-established cults. "Mithras? Isis? Dionysis? Dionysis would be a good one – plenty of wine goblets needed there. Permanently drunk, he is." I thought better of it. Those cults already had strict rules to be followed with no opportunity for imagination. "Or what local gods are worthy of devotion?"

"You want to convince the Celts to abandon how they've worshipped their own deities for thousands of years and to follow you without question?"

I dipped my head to concede the point. "Fair enough. But who we're worshipping is just a detail that we can work out later."

"It's a pretty big detail," came the voice from the corner.

"Shut up, Nux."

"If who you are worshipping is a detail for later," Tiber asked, "what are the details you need to work out first?"

"Administration. Location needs to be carefully considered – we need to draw in worshippers, so the temple needs to be somewhere visible. And initial funding, though the returns would be fast—"

"Returns? You're going to take advantage of worshippers?"

"Well, for one, I'm not taking advantage of them – they'll still get the full worship experience and they'll leave happy and fulfilled. Two, because they will be worshipping in a suitable manner, the gods will be placated. And three – why not? Everyone else does. Ever watched an augur at work?"

"And you don't think that's crass?" he asked.

"Auguries? Yeah, probably."

"No, I mean the primary motivation of your cult being your material benefit?"

"I'm not going to be charging for false positive auspice readings, if that's what you mean. It'll be genuine, but we'll control the ceremonial goods. No outside offerings allowed..." I was losing them, so like a good salesman, it was time to deflect attention. "At least I'll be more competent at it than Petronax – how in Hades does someone lose a body at a funeral?"

"Probably someone who thinks in terms of the 'full worship experience'. I don't think I've ever met such an impious devotee."

I felt my jaw stiffen and I jabbed the broom at the floor with renewed ferocity. I heard Nux snigger and I wondered if human sacrifice was big in this part of the world. Tiber's problem was that he lacked vision. He'd change his tone when he saw the benefits that priesthood could bring. I looked over at him as he scooped up his cloak for the walk home. It was old and worn but serviceable.

"Enica's killed a chicken for tonight," he called back as he walked out the door. "Be there in an hour if you want any."

Juno bless that woman. There were five reasons why Tiber could only afford one slave and an old cloak. I knew them as One, Two, Three, Four and Five but they probably had other names; Lucanus, Catia and the like.

They ranged in age between one and nine years old and to their credit they each helped their parents in some form or another. Number One, the eldest, was learning how to carve moulds for use in the workshop. They were acceptable enough, his nimble fingers being particularly adept at vines and foliage designs. Number Five, the youngest, helped clean the house by devouring dropped food, regardless of age, type, or stage of mummification.

They lived a frugal but stable existence, which allowed Enica to adopt occasional strays like myself for dinner once a week. Tiber's wife could weave together a feast out of scraps when she had to, let alone what she could conjure up when given proper ingredients, and they were always willing to share it with me.

I would make this cult work, if only to help raise that family up.

4

Tiber's household always ate early in the evening – the burden of parenthood – but still they lent me a lantern to find my way home. Getting home during the day was tricky. At night, I risked breaking an ankle.

It pained me to think it, but Nux was probably right. As I navigated the path downwards, I thought about which deity would be worthy of worship in my cult. It was a detail I could not leave unresolved for long.

Perhaps auguries were an avenue that I needed to explore further. Interpreting messages was certainly a reliable source of income, but what type of messages and which deity? Thunder and lightning, the tools of Jupiter?

No. Too well known and too tightly controlled. Everyone knew they had to keep Jupiter, the king of the gods, placated, but what we needed was a deity that no-one had considered cult-worthy before. One that we could sell as a powerful but slighted being on the warpath against humanity unless humanity flocked to us for help.

One whose messages came from the birds, perhaps? Again no, reading the flight of birds was a common enough practice which would encourage rival priests, which would drive down prices.

Reading quadrupeds was possible and less common. Perhaps that was the answer. We could start a cult of Epona, a Celtic fertility goddess and the protector of horses, but then we ran into the problem that Tiber had pointed out – we'd be telling the Celts how to worship their own goddess, and no-one would pay us to do that. I made a mental note to investigate possible eastern religions and cursed my luck that I no longer had access to my father's library. Tertia, dear sister, may need to become my research assistant, either willingly or else as the subject of my refined emotional blackmail techniques. That was probably unnecessary - I suspected that she would love to be involved in such a bizarre undertaking.

I had reached the point of my walk where the path began to level out, where the darkness under the tree canopy gave way to the narrow riverbank dotted with moonlit shelters. At that time of night you could mistake it for beauty, until that first stagnant whiff brought your romantic head firmly back to reality.

It was there that a noise interrupted my musing, a noise that made my blood freeze. Most people fear the sound of Cerberus, his multi-headed baying announcing their impending spiritual incarceration behind the gates of Hades, but even those ghouls damned to the lava of Tartarus had never heard what I heard that night.

The birds of the gods, rejected and dismissed, were screeching their discontent at being snubbed. Whether they were the owls of Minerva or the vultures of Mars, I couldn't tell (although in hindsight I could have ruled out the quails of Vulcan), but they were shrieking and their shrieks were resolving into words, and those words were...

They were...

"Get out of my house, you gods-cursed son of a harpy."

Jovina's door was flung open and the lamplight from within illuminated the path from the house to the fence. It was broken by the broad form of Augustalis as he was cast out.

"You keep your hands off her!" Jovina's angry voice really did raise itself about three octaves from her normal whine.

A bit of a non-sequitur, but the only way I could describe Jovina's normal 'not-really-angry-but-just-a-bit-peeved' level of whine is to compare her household to Tiber and Enica's. It is unbelievable how well Tiber's children settle down to their meals. Number Two helped to feed Number Five, while One, Three and even Four attacked their own meals with self-contained ferocity, allowing the adults to have a semi-civilised conversation. I don't have kids of my own and nor am I likely to any time soon, but the noises that I hear from Jovina's household at dinnertime suggest that someone was being brutally murdered each night.

I should have recognised her voice from previous instances of homicidal indigestion, but the added mania threw me off.

"You're getting paranoid, Jovina." Augustalis hollered back, his own voice revealing the strain he was under. "Nothing is changing. Be reasonable, for both your sakes!"

"Get out!"

I chuckled to myself in the dark. Jovina should be keen to claim Augustalis from his own wife now that Eratosthenes wasn't an issue anymore, but by casting him out she was no doubt pushing him back to her.

Jovina's ire was not placated merely by expelling her lover from the house, however. She had to send him off with a few parting blows with a short-handled broom, forcing him backwards off the threshold, at which point the door was slammed shut in his face. He pounded it with his fists but to no avail. Every word he yelled through the wood was over-pronounced and over-dramatic.

"You are not getting out of it that easily, Jovina. She's not happy. You know what that means. Let me in..."

I didn't fancy colliding with Augustalis on the path when he tired of his efforts. It was a narrow track and he had the physique of one who hoisted sacrificial sheep above his head with one arm for fun. As a heavy man, he was a contender for the future post of cult security guard, but right now it would not be a sound life choice to block his path on a dark night after he had been scorned.

I kept to the more overgrown patches on the path to soften the sound of my boots and slipped between the boulders unseen. While Jovina had invested in reasonable door locks, a stiff breeze could blow my own front door off its hinges. I put my shoulder to it and jostled the latch enough to shake it loose and forgo the need to find my key.

It's a weird feeling, arriving home and sensing that someone else is in the building with you, but I didn't need to reach for the fire poker. I put the lantern down and used its flame to light a few candles.

"Come on out, Pac," I called into the gloom that was my bedroom.

A few moments silence was followed by a shuffling sound as the forlorn boy edged his way out and into the light. He refused eye contact; his eyes, almost hidden by a fringe kept too long, were fixed on the corner of the floor behind me.

"How'd you know?"

I nodded towards Jovina's loaf of bread on my table. I had forgotten to take it over to her and it was now rock hard. Even so, a good chunk of it was missing. "It was either you or the biggest rats in the Empire have invaded my home again."

"Could've been a burglar."

"Who'd want to break into this hovel?"

Pacatus' eyes flicked upwards to meet mine at last, however briefly, with a slight lifting of the corner of his mouth.

"Come on," I stepped up to my kitchen bench and reached down for a sealed jug and two glasses from the back of the bottom shelf. "While you wait for the lovers' tiff to die down next door, at least you can enjoy some of this." I cracked open the seal and breathed in the peaty aroma that escaped from the confines of the jug.

"Lovers' tiff?"

"Augustalis and your mother."

"That's not..."

I looked up as his voice trailed off and he looked like he had been stung. I tried not to chuckle. "I'm sorry, lad. It must be hard thinking about your mother with anyone but your father. Or Eratosthenes, at least. Here," I passed him a glass of dark, syrupy liquid. He accepted it, revealing nails bitten down to the quick. He sniffed at the drink and pulled a face as if the liquid had been skimmed off the top of a cesspit by harpies.

"What is this?" he asked.

"I'd have thought that someone from Britannia would have known what 'beer' is."

"I know what beer is," he replied, still studying the drink with distrust, "but what is this?"

I rolled my eyes. "Just drink up." With my own drink in hand, I sank down onto my solitary dining couch. It was a glorious piece of furniture, which I had rescued in a dilapidated state from the top of a burn pile built up by a particularly austere but anonymous client in lieu of payment for a glass delivery. Not even the slaves had wanted it for their quarters, which I had thought was just insane.

I dubbed my prize the 'Lounge of Uncertainty,' in honour of the look of consternation that befell the face of anyone whose eyes drifted over its magnificence. Tiber had not been amused but it was my pride and joy; the one consolation that I had made to its repair being that the cushions now conformed perfectly to the contours of my body.

That left Pac with the only option but to perch on a stool - one of my 'Chairs of Despair.' As I watched him shift around, knowing that no stool could ever be comfortable, I realised how to placate Tiber and help Jovina without ever having to spend a single coin.

I would be a mentor for her eldest, on the cusp of manhood

despite his marble-smooth chin.

I took a sip of my drink and savoured the sensation of smoky, burnt malt on my tongue. "My own creation. I get the ingredients from Tiber - he fancies himself as a brewer too. But he doesn't think large scale. That's what you gotta do, lad. Always think large scale and one step ahead. That's what I do. That's why I bought this place."

"You thought big and bought yourself a soggy hovel?"

"Scoff if you like, but it's my fall-back if I can't make Tiber's glass business work. Beer. I'll grow my own ingredients – I'll shape the quagmire out the back into ditches to soak and grow the barley for malt. Then I'll produce my own beer to sell far and wide."

He looked confused. "But I've seen barley trenches. We went past them when we moved to Londinium. They're massive, if you want to make lots. You've got no room here."

I blinked. "When you moved to Londinium? I thought you grew up here?"

His eyes slid back to the corner of the room as his cheeks reddened. "No, I... we're from elsewhere."

"Where? Your mother's never mentioned it."

"Just from elsewhere, all right? Does it matter?"

"Okay, okay, it's fine." A thought occurred to me, in all its brilliant form. "You can help me, you know."

"What?"

"Digging trenches, raising the barley. The pay won't be, well... the pay will have to wait until our first sales come in but you'll have a stake in the business. We'll share the profit."

"Oh sod off, Calvus."

The outright rejection took me aback. No hesitation, no consideration of my proposal. Just a flat 'no'.

"Now come on," I started. "I'm offering you something most your age would never have, part ownership of a business.

You'd support your family, your mother can't look after you your whole life."

I'd struck a nerve. Before, he'd looked disgruntled. Now, his expression was positively dark.

"She's all right, you know. She does her best."

"I'm sure she does, but she needs help now. A reliable income. Did Eratosthenes have anything set aside to fall back on?"

Pac snorted. "Don't be stupid. There's nothing."

"There you go, then. You've got to start working."

He was cracking but still reluctant to see reason. "I'll not dig trenches. Haven't you got anything else? I'll clean your house for a fee."

"It doesn't need cleaning. I sweep once a month, that's about it."

"At your workshop, then?"

"Tiber has a slave for that."

"Oh."

He said no more and started to brood. I realised it had been too soon to broach the subject, so I decided to let it lie. No use in pushing the matter and having him dig his heels in. After a few moments, I spoke to break the silence.

"You know, it's big of you to admit that about your mum, as a growing lad. About the work she puts in. Most boys your age don't recognise it."

Pac's expression lightened as he relaxed a little. "Is your mum all right too?"

"Mine's dead."

"Oh. Sorry."

I waved away his concern. "It's all right. Happened years ago. You've lost two fathers now, so I don't think we need to make a competition of it. You can have my father if you want. We don't see eye to eye."

"What happened?"

I winked. "State secret."

He studied me.

"Did you become an actor?"

I blinked. "Why does everyone always think so little of me?"

He shrugged and looked away. "It's what I'd do. Become someone I'm not and hide who I really am."

I laughed. He'd learn. Even here I could not truly hide who I was – I was an educated Roman in the provinces, so I stood out from the crowd. I changed the subject. "So how did the rest of the funeral go?"

"It didn't. They couldn't find him."

"Eratosthenes? Surely that was just a matter of nipping over to the other funeral and trading biers?"

"He wasn't there."

"Wasn't there?"

"Or was already cremated. Or something. I don't know."

I shook my head. "Has anyone spoken to Petronax?"

"My mother had a few more words to say to him."

"I'll bet she did. But what about compensation? He hasn't given Eratosthenes the send off they paid for. Maybe Augustalis could go, they don't have to hide their relationship now—"

"Augustalis can keep the Hades out of it!" Pac leapt to his feet. "Things would just be better if he'd disappeared instead of Eratosthenes."

"Pac..."

He grabbed the remains of the stale bread.

"Thanks for this. I've got to go," he said as he disappeared out the door and into the night.

***

Curse me and my slim hold on decency. The next morning found me not at the workshop crafting the next superb perfume bottle or chalice to grace our shop shelves, nor scouting feasible temple sites for ritualistic glory.

It found me hiking, sweaty and annoyed, across the long bridge over the River Tamesis. If Pac was not yet ready to face the facts of life and earn a living, then the least I could do was to secure them some money to live off in the meantime.

That meant confronting Petronax to demand a refund. I rehearsed my irate, wronged customer speech as I walked, destined for the temple complex on the riverine islands south of the city.

I wasn't entirely disappointed by this turn of events. The temple to which I was destined was dedicated to Mars Camulus and the Imperial Cult. Construction had been completed mere weeks before and it was a new domain from which Petronax could lord it over his worshippers in ways far beyond the altar-in-the-wall type affair he had presided over previously. I was keen to see it, if only from the perspective of industrial espionage.

The road south ran straight through the centre of a growing settlement beyond the bridge, before passing through a narrow isthmus and into the southern outskirts of town. It was choked with traffic. I heard the ceremony at the temple before I saw it and as the road made a sweeping bend around a row of trees, it fell into view. The temple itself was a narrow but tall square tower surrounded at its base by a covered verandah. The paved yard outside was playing host to the event, during which the worshippers (of which there were many) had their ears bombarded by a cacophony of bells, cymbals, rattles and pipes.

Ditches had been dug around the entire precinct, funnelling visitors through a single point of access watched over by two of Petronax's robed assistants.

If you can imagine the look that people might cast towards a fullery slave as he emerged from the urine-soaked depths of a laundry vat, then you know the look that the assistants threw to me now – as if I looked clean at a distance but the whiff of something acrid floated before me as I approached. They blocked my path and a glance behind them made me feel distinctly under-dressed and under-prepared for the situation. Everyone within was decked out in their finest togas, military cloaks or silken stolas, with not a single drab tunic to be seen.

What ensued was a dreadfully mimed conversation as I frantically signed that I wanted to enter and the elder of the pair yelled futilely in my direction, unable to make himself heard over the noise of the ceremony. I didn't need to hear his voice; his manner was less than welcoming, and more "does-not-play-well-with-plebs".

The panicked sounds of a bull joined the crescendo before both the racket and the bellowing abruptly vanished.

"—late!" The old man shouted into the silence. His face flushed and he turned to look behind him. That was all the distraction that I needed. I ducked under his elbow and hurried into the crowd before he was able to recover.

I mingled my way through the outer edge of the gathering. Petronax was at the front, joined today by a pudgy middle-aged man whose hair only existed in tufts around his ears and whose arms were covered in blood up to his shoulders. He had taken mere seconds to slice open the bull's carcass to deliver forth the still-throbbing offal.

He was a haruspex, and as haruspex it was his job to examine the entrails to determine what mood the gods were in. I wondered to which deity of the jointly consecrated temple they were communing with at this particular event and if the deity honoured would be favourable towards those gathered. If it was Mars Camulus, it was anyone's guess; the god of war could be tempted to ignite the flames of conflict just to alleviate boredom.

If it was one of the deified Emperors, the outcome might be equally as dismal. Upon their deaths, many of the previous

Roman Emperors to date had been lifted to the status of godhood, but I imagined that any of those Emperor-gods who had been poisoned or stabbed by assassins would not be looking down too favourably on the living under any circumstances.

In reality, most of the Emperors to date had been poisoned or stabbed by assassins, so the future looked bleak for all of us.

Petronax and his guest of honour were busy examining the ligaments of the liver, so while I waited for my chance to draw Petronax aside I inspected the setup that he had acquired for himself. Nobody paid me any attention as I ducked between the columns of the temple to inspect the building itself. The first thing I noticed seemed to be the most important. It was an inscription set into the wall:

To the Divinities of the Emperors and to the god Mars Camulus. Tiberinius Celerianus, a citizen of the Bellovaci, moritix, of Londoners the first...

It waffled on in that manner but that was a definite must for my own temple. An inscription naming me as its benefactor. I looked over to the crowd and wondered which was Celerianus. I fancied that he was the Gallic-looking one front and centre over there, with the bearing of demigod standing proud in his reddish-bordered toga.

The doors of the temple were thrown open to let the statues inside witness the sacrifices made in their honour. I dared not go in – I would have been ripped apart by an angry mob for breaching the inner sanctum, but I saw enough through the opening of the bright red room inside. There was Mars in all his military splendour, a ten-foot-tall statue of painted wood standing silently in a cloud of good intentions and frankincense. I fancied that he was rather relieved for the breath of fresh air the ceremony gave to him, or else having his appetite piqued by the true aroma of love and peace that even my olfactory senses could now detect floating in our direction.

Spit roast.

The first was already sizzling away nicely as I rounded the back of the temple, and bore the carcass of a ram while the two young slaves loaded up a pig onto the second – the first of the sacrifices that had been made earlier that morning. They saw my plain dress and, assuming I was some attendant or unimportant observer, showed no objection to my approach. Together, unseen by the official contingent of worshippers, we sampled meat from all parts of the ram's body as it cooked. Without fail, it was tender and juicy and sweet, a divine gift from a placated god. Perhaps the Emperors of years past weren't as hung up on the ill manner of their deaths as much as I had imagined.

"This is something else," I complimented the boys on their handiwork. "You two are fast, I can't imagine these beasts died more than an hour ago and you've already got them skinned and dressed and on the fire. The ram looks half done."

They snorted and gave each other the supercilious looks of those who feel they are far more worldly and knowledgeable than the rest of us. I had seen that look all too often at my father's dinners, where he would play the role of obsequious gourmand, blind to the fact that his guests could afford to dye their meals saffron yellow at home, well above our modest cumin offerings. I supposed that knowing looks cast between temple slaves were the bravest form of rebellion they could afford.

"Check this out," one of them said, keen to show off. He showed me a large trap door behind the temple, hidden amongst potted plants. He pushed them aside and opened it enough for me to glance inside. The air that emerged was cool and moist.

"There's your animals from today," he said, pointing to the two freshly killed carcasses in the centre of the cellar, hanging from the ceiling in the gloom, blood still dripping from their severed necks into large basins underneath.

"I don't understand. If they're today's sacrifice, then what's out there?"

The boy laughed. "Animals we killed a week ago, of course."

That was in no way an explanation.

"If we cooked today's animals," he continued, "they'd be tough. We can't have people going around thinking that chewy meat was a sign of cranky gods. We're best off killing a ram and a pig ahead of time and letting them hang for a week first. Something about letting it hang in the dark makes the meat tender. Succulent meats all around from generous gods."

"The meat doesn't spoil in the meantime?"

"Oh no. That's how we know the gods approve. We can keep a carcass down here for a couple of weeks, no problem."

I could almost hear Tiber's voice in my head and cursed him for it. Petronax was embarked on a level of deception that I knew would rankle with him. "But people would be expecting to eat the animals they just saw killed."

He shrugged. "So?"

He made a good point. This was brilliant. Even I had to admire Petronax' audacity, despite whatever else could be said about him. Everyone would leave contentedly full after this evening's feast. If the gods didn't care, why should we? I decided there and then that my future temple needed a cellar. I wondered for how much Petronax would sell these two boys to me - their butchery knowledge would be invaluable.

The proceedings had drawn to a close as we returned and I melted back into the crowd, now spreading throughout the complex, renewing old acquaintances or seeing to their personal needs now that the long ceremony was over, leaving behind dry throats and full bladders. Petronax was being sociable, ingratiating himself with members of his congregation, and I had to remember the reason why I was there in the first place. He had won my begrudging respect with the meat switch, but he had left a friend destitute and hungry. I couldn't let myself lose sight of that. Already, only a few words of my well-rehearsed irate customer speech came back to mind as I tried to recall them, so I took the first opportunity I could to attract his eye. When I did, that eye squinted at me.

"I know you."

I nodded. He had an accent I couldn't place and the slight, twitchy mannerisms of a short-sighted shrew. "Laelius Calvus. I'm a friend of Jovina. I was a friend of Eratosthenes."

I was expecting some sort of disgruntled or embarrassed noise to emerge from his lips, but quite the opposite occurred. His face lifted into a broad smile.

"Oh, then you'll be here about the Funeral Club."

"Well, yes, but perhaps not in the way you think."

"Come, let me show you."

He spun on his heel and hurried away, not checking to see if I followed. After a few moments, when I could come up with no better plan, I went after him. So much for bravado in the face of tyranny and greed. It took mere moments to turn me into a compliant little puppy dog, trotting along at his heels.

He led me across the yard to an outbuilding nearby. Unlike the temple, the room he took me to was simple and strictly business. A long table ran down the middle, devoid of decoration, and a cupboard stood at the far corner, its doors latched closed. Petronax gestured me to one side of the table while he strode down the other side and approached the cupboard. He turned to face me.

"Tell me, what happens when you die?" His brown eyes did not blink as he awaited my response. They were captivating – one pupil was bigger than the other, permanently dilated, but whether through injury or touch of the gods, I couldn't tell.

"Um," I mentally shook myself to break out of the spell. "Well, my business partner will have to work more to pick up the slack, my neighbour will steal the glassware from my house before vagrants take over, and my father will throw a party—"

"No, no, no," he flicked his hand in dismissal. "To you. What happens to you when you die?"

"I'm not sure I understand."

"Do you go to the Great Below, does the transmigration of your soul need assistance to reach its next form, does your Ka and Ba separate from your Khet to enjoy existence in the Land of Two Fields and watch over your family respectively?"

"An afterlife?" I blew air from my cheeks. "Well, I guess I hope to arrive in the fields of Elysium, but knowing my luck I'll be relegated to the Asphodel Meadows." No eternal bliss for me, just the mundanities given by Pluto to the indifferent and ordinary souls. Unless, of course, my cult worked. That would demand the respect of any god, underworldly or otherwise.

He turned his attention to a cupboard in the corner. "Ah, one of those."

"What do you mean, 'one of those'?"

"Oh," he looked back, surprised that he had seemed to cause some offence. "A Roman, of course. I offer a fully customised service..." he reached past an Anubis priest mask on a shelf to pull out a model of a bier and half a dozen miniature Roman funerary masks and placed them on the table between us. "No matter what your background or afterlife beliefs - Roman, Celtic, Parthian or Egyptian, I can modify the Funeral Club service to suit any need. Now, I'm sure a Roman as noble as yourself has considered the need for a death mask to pass on to your descendants, to add to their veritable collection of distinguished ancestors."

To demonstrate, he picked up the most ornate mini mask - a carving of a bald middle-aged man who, even at a squint, bore little resemblance to me.

The Laelii haven't been a big name in the history of Rome. The only branch worth mentioning are the Laelius Balbii.

Balbus, of course, meaning 'beard'. When the Laelius Calvii started, someone with a weird sense of humour must have wanted to distance themselves from the Balbii. 'Calvus' means bald, despite every Calvus I'm aware of having a full head of dark hair.

"You don't know who I am, how do you know about my ancestors?" I asked.

"Doesn't every Roman claim to come from distinguished ancestors?"

"What if I told you I came from a long line of professional armpit hair pluckers?"

"Then, perhaps a pair of tweezers adorning your gravestone? Now," he continued, unfazed by my purported profession. "My mask artist is adept at creating durable plaster moulds that will last your family for generations. You'll need that – each of your noble offspring and their children will want a copy of your visage adorning their halls. We will prepare this for you while you are still at your peak physical condition." He glanced at me with an appraising look. "We'd best get on to that as soon as possible."

Cheeky sod. I frowned. "I think you are getting ahead of yourself. I didn't—"

"Yes, of course. You would be interested in prices—"

"No, not really."

"Oh good." He positively beamed now. "Then let's discuss quality of service."

"Yes, let's. Did Eratosthenes have a mask created? I don't remember seeing it during the funeral procession."

A crack appeared in Petronax's warm smile.

"He paid for another type of service. A plaster cast wasn't required."

"And neither was it a requirement that his body be available for his own funeral?"

The smile faded all together and Petronax placed the model in his hand back on the table.

"Why are you really here?" he asked.

"I'm here on behalf of Jovina, protecting her interests."

Petronax looked confused. "Jovina sent you?"

"Um, yes." Petronax raised an eyebrow. "Well, no. I'm a thoughtful neighbour. She and her husband paid for a service they did not receive. She's lost her support and family income. Her son is reduced to eating mouldy bread and you need to make restitution for failing them and leaving them broke."

"But I have."

"What?"

Petronax rolled his eyes before explaining to me in a tone that implied I was five years old whilst at the same time sounded like it was a line learned rote from a contract. "I refunded Jovina the remittance they paid for the bronze-level funeral service as it was unable to be completed due to extenuating circumstances. And more, by way of an apology and in good faith."

I didn't know what to say to that. What was Pac thinking, implying that they had been left with nothing? I scratched my eye, trying to work out how to get out of there without looking like a complete idiot.

"So where did the money go?" I asked, not actually intending to say it out loud.

"Perhaps you should ask Jovina that. So, are you going to sign up to the Club or not?"

5

"**I** have an appointment next week to have a mould made of my face."

Tiber roared with laughter. Even Nux bit his lip in a vain attempt to stay in control, the swish of his broom becoming decidedly more jerky as he swept up slivers of glass from the warehouse floor.

"So, you signed up for that crap?" he asked.

"Not the full service. Just the mask. I'm going to send it to my father for Saturnalia."

Tiber and Nux both collapsed at that. At least they could see the funny side but it niggled away at me until I abandoned the two of them categorising tools that I couldn't put a name to and stomped off home to confront Pac. I was determined to find out why he had let me make a fool of myself.

The little...

His embellishment of the truth was more disappointing than...

When I saw him, I'd...

Jovina answered my hammering at the door, interrupting my poetic internal rant. Her eyes were red and puffy and when she spoke she sounded blocked up.

"What do you want, Calvus?"

"I... ah..."

She sighed. "You might as well come in, then."

Now, I have a loose interpretation of what constitutes 'clean', but what I saw when I stepped across the threshold took my breath away and again I can only describe it by comparing it to the only other family who will tolerate me inside their home. Tiber and Enica's house looked lived in: essentially clean other than a sea of wooden blocks, bone whistles and a range of dolls cut, stitched and stuffed from old clothes. These were all swept indiscriminately into the corner with the speed, skill and resignation of a mother accustomed to fighting the toy tide at least six times a day. It was the house of a family who looked after themselves but felt the pressure of simply being a large, young family.

Jovina's house looked like she had given up. Under the broken toys and food scraps, layers of muck were tracked over the wooden floor and mildew was building up on the corners of the kitchen bench. Unwashed plates were crammed into a bucket of brown water. Clothes were abandoned where they were shed. Numerous cups of half-drunk, vinegar-grade wine were abandoned around the room, several of which had tipped over and disgorged their contents across furniture and baby clothes alike, leaving an acidity hanging in the air that my nose hairs objected to.

"Wow..."

"Oh yeah, like your place is always immaculate."

"I'm a single, slave-less man living in a swamp. Of course it's not. But your place... this... what's the matter?"

She slumped onto a stool.

"I have lost a husband, you know."

"Yeah, but..."

"But what?"

Now, here is where you would expect diplomacy to kick in and platitudes to be uttered to a recently widowed mother on the verge of some kind of brain snap. But not from me. I was too well educated for that.

"But you didn't even cry at his funeral," I said. "If anything, you took the opportunity to desecrate a corpse."

My cheeks flushed even as the words left my mouth. Here's the thing about being educated. My boyhood was spent with my nose almost touching the recto of a scroll, studying dry literature selected by my father. My father, who thought that knowing that the inside of a scroll was called a 'recto' would be more useful in day-to-day life than knowing how to console a friend.

She looked up and glared at me. "You can be a real jerk sometimes, Calvus."

"Sorry."

An uncomfortable silence ensued, but astoundingly she didn't kick me out. I think she wanted just not to be alone, to have some sort of human contact, however distasteful the conversation. My eyes wandered around the room. There was one object that was impeccably maintained, a shining beacon in the chaos: the family shrine.

Set into the centre of the back wall, its display included a handful of figurines of the Lares, the spirits that protected the household. They stood around the shrine, their windblown tunics frozen in bronze, bearing cornucopia aloft as if they were holding the precious vessels up out of the surrounding detritus. Several of Eratosthenes' Egyptian deities of choice loitered at the back. The animal-headed gods had been pushed aside - not Jovina's preference for devotion but also not completely shunned. Who knew what devious revenge a slighted theriocephalic deity could concoct?

Pride of place was given over to Minerva. Her statuette form reclined on a pedestal, her helmet tipped back to reveal her face. She leant on her spear as if resting from a long day strategising for the demise of her unwanted suitors, then healing their stab wounds before inspiring satires to be written in their honour. The Roman goddess led a full and busy life. Her alabaster chiffon was stained blood red, whether as a fashion choice or the outcome of a righteous war or gruesome healing procedure, I wouldn't hazard to guess.

When I turned around, Jovina had pulled one knee up on

her stool and was hugging it while staring at the shrine. Her voice was so small when she spoke.

"She thinks I've forsaken her."

"Who?"

"Sulis."

No elaboration was given. That was a level of optimistic naivety that I couldn't account for in Jovina's otherwise observant personality. Who the Hades was Sulis? Only one answer came to mind.

"Well, she might need to accept that Augustalis wants to be with you now. It sounds like their marriage is failing anyway. "

"What?"

"Sulis. If she's a true friend to you, then she'll accept that everyone will be happier this way. If she doesn't, you're better off without her."

Well, at least she stopped crying. Now, she stared at me as if I was a few horses short of a chariot race.

"Bloody Romans," she swore.

"What?"

"You lot spend your existence renaming everyone's gods because your memories can't cope," her voice bordered on manic now. "Give someone a new look or a new name, and you suddenly can't see who they are any more. Minerva. Sulis is Minerva. They are one and the same. Sulis Minerva."

I blinked. "Oh, that makes more sense."

"Gah," she threw a hand in my direction and gave up. As she sunk back into silent sullenness, one very important question came to mind, the only question that I could possibly think to ask in such a situation.

"Why do you call her Sulis?"

What? You thought that I would ask her why she had allegedly forsaken a goddess? I'm tactless, but not completely horrible. Confronting her about it would not make her tell me her life story. But, lulling her into a false sense of security might.

"Sulis has been worshipped here for centuries, long before the Romans arrived. Her temple..." her eyes glazed over as her mind went elsewhere. "Her temple, at Aquae Sulis. A place of love and worship, of healing and cleanliness. There's a bathhouse connected to her temple for healing the sick. She is such a giving goddess, so caring."

"You've visited there?" She didn't answer me as she continued to stare at the shrine. "A goddess of healing and cleanliness?" I tried to refrain from letting my eyes roam around the room, but I did not have to wonder about why Jovina may no longer be welcome there.

"Water comes forth from her sacred spring. There is... something within it. People travel great distances to visit her here, to drink or swim within the waters. It rejuvenates people, people who are sick or injured. Sulis cares for them."

A thought occurred to me. "Is that where you moved from? Pac mentioned—"

She snapped out of her reverie. "Oh, mind your own business, Calvus." Now there was the Jovina I recognised. The screech was back, which was just as well, I had been starting to wonder if she herself was sick. "What do you want, anyway?"

"Actually, I came looking for Pac. Why did he tell me you had no money?"

"What?"

"He came to see me. Well, he came to hide in my house while you were having your little heart-to-heart with Augustalis last night. He implied... no, he told me that you had no money. That you were desperate."

Jovina stiffened, her expression dark.

"He had no right to speak to you about that."

"He didn't have too. Poor kid was starved, he was happy to get his hands on the mouldy old crusty bread that you yourself said you needed me to get. I'm trying to help you."

"I don't need help."

"Well, I thought you did. I went to see Petronax to get you a refund for his shoddy service."

Her face paled. "You did what?"

I stepped away from the shrine towards her and my foot slid on a baby's ragdoll on the floor. Its wine-stained face stared up with what I imagined to be a plaintive expression. I could feel my voice becoming dangerously low.

"What happened to the money he gave you, Jovina? Just why do your kids starve in a filthy hovel while you enjoy life with Augustalis? Or is he headed back to his own wife now that your affair isn't quite so deliciously illicit?"

"Get out of my house—"

"You gods-cursed son of a harpy?" I finished her sentence.

I ducked just in time; the bowl Jovina aimed at my head smashed on the wall next to me as I made a break for the door.

***

'Voyage, travel and change impart vigour.'

Seneca the Younger wrote that, and I credit it as the source of all the tension between me and my father. Had my father realised that my expensive and yet oh-so-disinterested tutor only ever came to life when he spoke of Seneca and his other radical gems of thought, such as using wealth to help others, he may have hired someone different. I think that my tutor might have even painted images of the philosopher on the walls of his abode - pout, jowls and all - like some sort of demented fanatic.

He should have stuck to garden scenes and orgies, like everybody else.

But, the concept of getting out and about had claimed a small part of my scroll-bound mind, and came to life every time

I needed to revel in rebellion against Father. If an interview with a potential legal mentor awaited, the wine-soaked hills of the Campania called. If a treatise on economic sea trade appeared in my vicinity, the salty docks of Ostia beckoned. I classed my escapades as educational field trips. Father called them belligerence.

Now years later, and the lure of a field trip was again causing tension. Tiber announced this to the world as he hollered his displeasure at my back as I trotted away from the workshop astride a hired donkey.

The state of her house had opened up my nostrils, and her behaviour had opened up my eyes, but Jovina's description of the Temple of Sulis Minerva had opened up my mind. I mean that figuratively, of course, even though Jovina had tried to do so in the literal sense with flying crockery.

But, her reverence of Sulis, and the possibilities she had revealed in her description of the sacred springs - it was astounding. I had thought of religion as temples, marble, and paint. I should not be so narrow minded. Why restrict my cult to traditional temples and altars? At Aquae Sulis, they had found a goddess in a bath.

My future patrons might find a deity in a dining hall, or the immortal in a latrine. Or, best yet, the holy in a market stall. One selling divine challises made of glass. Petronax might have a temple complex at his fingertips, but I would have a temple shopping precinct under my control.

At Aquae Sulis, they could show me how. I just had to get there first but that proved problematic.

I called my rented ignoble steed Marcus. I'm pretty sure that's Petronax's first name, and Petronax is an ass. Unlike his namesake and against all expectations, Marcus was a delight. He even came with a younger brother in tow. I used the extra beast to carry supplies, so I called him Tractus. Marcus and Tractus were well trained, gentle and had more stamina than I thought possible of any animal in existence.

They were not my problem.

My problem was one of perception. Getting drunk in the woods and staying in one spot until the sun rises is technically known as camping, right? I mean, the legions have a different definition, but I had a fire starter kit and vague instructions from an ex-legionary donkey merchant about how to make a lean-to shelter, so I don't see how what I was doing was any different from how the Roman military might take its evening rest. Just smaller scale, that's all.

Camping is not all that it's cracked up to be. Unless you have a full staff, a commissary tent and latrines dug by the lower ranks, then it can be downright Hades.

The shelter fell over.

Twice.

I almost set my own boot on fire.

And, in my beer-addled state, every knot in a tree trunk became a blue-woad face and every firefly glimmer became the glint off a sharpened axe.

When I arrived at the first true stop, the town of Calleva Atrebatum, I was dehydrated and smelled like a wet donkey. By the time I reached Aquae Sulis, five days later, I looked like the love child between a faun and the Medusa, who hadn't inherited the human qualities of either. It left me with a dilemma. Should I find somewhere to stay, scrub up the best I could and visit the temple in the morning as a semi-clean potential partner? Or head straight there and put their bath service to the considerable test? I opted for the latter. Tonight, I would be in the tender hands of barbers and manicurists. Tomorrow, I would meet the priests and acolytes. The two were worlds apart, they would not associate a travel-worn mule merchant with the worldly sophisticate that would grace the morning's dedications.

I arranged for accommodation for myself, Marcus and Tractus at the first stable I came across near the edge of town and entered the town proper on foot. I've never been within a Roman town quite like Aquae Sulis. Everyone lived outside the town walls. As I made my way south, it all started out as you would expect - a baker, a laundry, houses and a carpenter's yard. Women carried babies in their arms and slaves ran errands. Some kid on the street corner was selling handfuls of foraged berries from a basket hooked over his elbow. I glanced in as I passed and I hoped he had a better botanical knowledge than I did - I recognised blackberries and raspberries, but mixed in with those was a red, semi-translucent, grape-like berry that could have been anything. I opted not to take him up on his offer of a cheap snack and moved on.

Ahead lay an earthen rampart with a gate built in across the roadway. The gates were wide open, allowing a steady stream of visitors to pass both ways. Once through, however, the entire atmosphere of Aquae Sulis changed and became... not heavier, but more reverent. People didn't whisper as they spoke to their friends, but neither did they shout. No houses abutted the street, but rather there was an array of public buildings, gardens and plazas carefully built so as not to outshine the monumental complex a couple of hundred metres up the road: the sacred springs of Sulis Minerva, and the accompanying temples and bathhouse.

I could see their roofs almost immediately - the pointed, triangular roof of the Roman temple, the domed vaults of the bathhouse adjacent, both bathed in orange light as the sun neared the horizon. I had thought of Londinium as the Roman Empire in city form, but inside the walls of Aquae Sulis was just Rome. Classical, marbled Rome, but without all those pesky tradespeople and smelly dwellings. If you want to sell the greatness of Roman civilisation to the Celts in its purest form, you show them the Forum and the Capitaline Hill, not the seedy underbelly of the Subura.

As I neared the first major intersection, a right turn would have taken me past a theatre to the temple precinct. That would be my route tomorrow, and indeed some in the crowd in which I walked forked off in that direction. Forewarned by the stable owner, I continued south to the next intersection, before turning and walking past the giant walls of the bathhouse to its entrance on the western side.

I paid in advance for a week's worth of visits and refused the offer of a hired slave to watch over my belongings while I bathed. No-one would want to go near my travel clothes in their current state; their stench was a thief deterrent stronger than any bored hireling would ever be.

Never have I found undressing to be more awkward. Upon being ushered into the changing rooms, nigh-on a dozen pairs of eyes fell upon me. Slaves lined the walls of the room, each guarding their little pocket of space within the compartments containing their master's belongings. I found a corner that was free, aware of the fact that I had the most attentive audience watching me undress than I've ever had. Londinium had bathhouses, but more often than not I merely grabbed a bucket filled from the river behind my house and used that to scrape myself off, or in the summer months I took a dip. Back in Rome, I frequented the seedier of the bathing establishments, those who's patrons could not afford a slave of their own and put their trust in the bathhouse's single security slave. Surely that was a much more economical choice than a slave for every loincloth?

As I tugged at my belt, I heard a gruff chuckle and glanced around. A wrinkled, old prune of a man stood beside me, his tunic looking as rough as mine.

"Don' mind the creepy spectator cohort, you've not got nothing they've never seen before." He stood uncomfortably close to me and started to strip, thrusting the crutch that he had hooked under his arm into my chest. "Here, hold this."

"Ah, thanks," I replied. "Somehow I get less self-conscious in a room filled with other men getting naked together than around those standing about fully dressed."

"Men getting naked together don' make eye contact," he said, whipping his tunic over his head and dropping his loincloth to the floor with unnatural speed. Then, he made eye contact. "You getting undressed or not? Come on, leave that there" – he nodded at the crutch – "and follow me."

Without his crutch, his gait was unusually lopsided. As he strode, his right hip would drop and his torso would lurch to the left. I yanked my own tunic over my head, crammed it into an empty compartment and followed him into the next room.

He didn't see me watching his hips, but he assumed correctly and answered the question I didn't have the guts to ask.

"Took an arrow to the butt, ten years back. Spent three weeks face down on a bed with my arse in the air. Been coming here almost every day since. At first I was hoping the great Sulis Minerva would heal me. She hasn't seen fit to, so now I just come each day to wee in her pool." I bit my lip, a move that he sneered at. "Don' worry. There's not much in reserve at the moment. If you're precious about it, I'll warn you first and you can swim away a few feet."

"Thanks."

We had entered the tepidarium, the warm bath designed to ease oneself into the heat before progressing on to the hot room. To me, as a Roman, it seemed standard enough, if a little larger than normal, and it currently played host to four other men, spaced around the edges of the pool before us, with their elbows hooked over the side.

"I'm Varro-with-the-gimpy-leg," my new friend said. "Not to be confused with Varro-with-one-eye and Varo-with-one-R-

and-the-nasty-cough."

"Well then, Varro-with-the-gimpy-leg, I'm Calvus-with-the-confused-look-on-his-face."

"First time here?"

"Yeah."

"Then forget about these rooms, these ain't what you've come to see." He did an about-face, or as best as he could manage, and lurched back to the changing room and through a different door to the frigidarium, a rectangular room with a circular, decidedly cold plunge pool that was normally the last stop on any visit to the baths. Even then he did not stop, making his way diagonally across the room to a door in the far corner.

"This is what you've come to see," he said, gesturing the doorway. I cocked my head and stepped through to something that I had never seen before in any bathhouse I'd visited. The room we entered was easily thirty metres long and half as wide, under a massive barrel-vaulted ceiling high above our heads. The biggest pool I had ever seen filled the floor-space. A steady plume of steam rose off the warm water into the cool air, taking on the pinky-orange hues of the setting sun, which was aided by the surrounding candelabras that were being lit against the dying light. The effect caused the bathers gathered at the far side of the pool, men and women both, to appear hazy and mystical to my eyes.

Archways lined the long sides of the pool, providing access to private nooks within which to sit and relax, converse or enjoy a massage. The vaulted ceiling was open at either end and supported by columns, allowing steam to escape but also allowing a variety of pigeons and starlings to flock and swirl above us, and find suitable roosts along the architraves.

Perhaps Varro-with-the-gimpy-leg's bladder reserves were not the worst problem one would face in this pool. Occasional plopping sounds heralded something much worse.

Varro-with-the-gimpy-leg pushed his way around me as I gaped, and eased himself down the steps into the water. The lines that marked his face relaxed as his body floated and he took a moment to enjoy the sensation. "You'll be back with us in a moment," he said. "Then, come on in, the water's lovely."

Denied the use of the tepidarium to acclimatise myself to the heat, stepping into the hot pool took my breath away. But, as Varro-with-the-gimpy-leg was now floating on his back with one eye open and fixed on me, I was determined not to show discomfort. I waded in. It was deep; if I let the tips of my toes touch the bottom, stretched and craned my neck so that I looked straight up at the ceiling, I could just about keep my nose above water, but a slight surge from someone diving in nearby would have sent me spluttering.

We bobbed along in companionable silence for a time. When we did speak, I spoke of glass-blowing and he related what he believed to be humorous, but thoroughly questionable stories from his years in the legions. The light from the sun disappeared completely and the candelabra created pockets of illumination around the room. The birds settled, and with them went my sense of trepidation. I took a few sips of the water in the hopes that its healing powers would continue to work from the inside to ease my achy muscles, and hoped beyond hope that the metallic twang of its flavour was caused by a gift from the goddess and not a gift from Varro-with-the-gimpy-leg.

"You one of them religious lot?" came Varro-with-the-gimpy-leg's voice in the dark.

"That's a rather personal question. Why do you ask?"

"You're making a noise like one of them religious lot."

"Noise?"

"Humming. Sighing. It's the same noise that lot make when they believe Sulis can be bothered to personally see to their needs."

I hadn't even realised I had made a sound. "Just enjoying the warmth."

"Yeah, right."

Silence returned. As I drifted, the masseuse shift change took place within the alcoves and I cringed on behalf of his victim at the renewed vigour of the new masseuse, with the energy to dig his fingers in with toe-curling ferocity. While watching the pain endured for an ambiguous amount of gain, a thought popped into my head.

"Why don't you think Sulis Minerva has healed you?" I asked. Varro-with-the-gimpy-leg snorted.

"You saw how I walk."

"Yeah, but while we've been in this pool, you've been swimming along like the best of them."

"So, you're saying as long as I never leave the pool, I'm fine? What sort a' life's that?" He flicked his hand into the water, sending a spray across my face. I blinked and rubbed my eyes but it did not change my train of thought.

"But what sort of life would you have led had you not been coming here?" I paddled backwards out of his splash zone as I spoke. "Maybe what you have is far better than what it could have been."

"Now you do sound like one of them lot. What would have happened otherwise? Would my legs have fallen off?"

"Maybe. By necessity, under the surgeon's blade."

"Sulis has no more reason to look after me personally than she does anyone else here, whether they be injured old farts like me, or cranky young idiots like the rest of them."

"Cranky young idiots?"

"Follow me."

He glided over to the edge, where his gracefulness came to an end and he clambered and lurched his way up the steps with the assistance of a nearby attendant. Varro-with-the-gimpy-leg led the way back to the frigidarium. This time, instead of continuing elsewhere, he approached three windows on the wall nearest us and cracked open the shutters so that we could peer through.

Beneath us was the Sacred Spring of Sulis Minerva itself, its waters sparsely lit, catching glints of light from nearby lamps. The edges of the spring had been lead-lined to form an oval-shaped pool, surrounded by a tiled platform. Beyond the spring stretched a plaza with an outdoor altar, and to the left stood the Temple of Sulis Minerva, both awash in firelight, pockets of illumination in the dark.

On the far side of the spring stood four people, spaced apart from each other, dressed in dark clothes as if in mourning. They each clutched something small against their chest, chanting inaudibly. As each finished their chant, they reached out and dropped their little package into the water, where it immediately sank out of sight. If they had noticed us above them, watching on, they didn't show it.

"What are they doing?" I asked Varro-with-the-gimpy-leg.

"Shirking responsibility."

I pulled away from the window and looked at him.

"They've each got some sort a grievance against someone who should of known better," he continued. "Someone stole their gloves, or their ring, or their cloak. Someone insulted them, or sneezed in their general direction. So now, rather than deal with it like the adults that they are, they ask the goddess to do it for them. Knew a man once who cursed his sister-in-law to horrible, terrifying diarrhoea because she broke a vase. Said it had been in his family for generations, but personally I think that sometimes accidents just happen."

I looked back out as a young girl released another item into the water.

"So, what are they dropping?" I asked.

"Written instructions, scratched into lead sheets for posterity. Minerva's got quite a to-do list piling up down there."

We watched as the next few people trundled over clutching their crumpled lead sheet. My eyes drifted in the direction from which they had approached, to where a table had been set up for a scribe to help the would-be cursers to scratch out their thoughts.

Of course, such help was only provided after they had dropped a significant pile of coins into the awaiting bucket off to the side.

I wondered if the value of those coins would be more or less than the value of the lost item for which they sought restitution, and if they would have been better spent on buying a replacement. While I tried to at least work out if the coins were of bronze or silver, an opportunity presented itself in such a way that only the divine could have foreseen. Behind the scribe, watching on with an air of mystery, stood a man I recognised. A pudgy, middle-aged man whose hair existed only in tufts around his ears, whom I had last seen standing beside Petronax and covered in the sacrificial blood of a bull.

Anyone entering the frigidarium behind us, sighting our two bare backsides (one well-toned, the other wrinkled and floppy, and both animated by the warm, flickering glow of numerous lamps positioned around the room as we lurked at the window), would have no idea that an entire religion had just burst into life inside my mind, like the birth of Minerva herself, and with it my strategy for getting inside the inner workings of the Temple of Sulis Minerva.

6

The birth of a new religion causes a flurry of brain activity that will keep you up all night, but it was worth it. By the next morning, there was no question that my future friends at the Temple of Sulis Minerva could throw at me for which I did not have an answer.

I repeated my previous day's walk through Aquae Sulis and turned down a breakfast of suspiciously cheerful red berries. I passed through the giant gates and took the first turn towards the temple. This approach took me through an open plaza, currently playing host to a thriving craft market, which would have been in the shadow of the temple of their patron goddess had it not been a morning market and the temple lay to the west.

Carpenters demonstrated the sturdiness of their stools by planting their own gruff backsides at the rear of their stalls, and from which they would refuse to move for any person until cash was flashed. Tanners created a mountain of hides, and woe betide anyone who wanted one that was not within the first four on top.

It was the spinners and weavers who knew their business. A picturesque rainbow of movement from displays of yarns and cloth draped in the breeze was revealed to be the lure for the sales trap. Should a wanderer's eyes fall upon them for even the briefest instant, the trap was sprung and their path would be blocked by the bait's creator, having lain in wait for just such a moment with their spiel.

Being waylaid in a labyrinthine mess of hawkers was not conducive to my plans, so I fell back upon old advice from my father, of all people.

"You've got every right to be there," he had told me as he

53

thrust me forward into some high-up social gathering or another, filled with people whose sedan chairs cost more than our entire house. "Just don't show them that you are nervous. Be confident, and they'll accept you as one of their own." It almost worked, too, until they saw that my retinue - my loyal followers whose job it was to trail around behind me and lend me an air of grandeur - consisted of two loaned slaves and my jowl-loving tutor.

But, through a busy marketplace, Father's advice would prove sound. Eyes forward, marching as if I owned the place, I remained unaccosted. I didn't break stride as I approached the columned entrance to the temple courtyard. I passed through, not stopping until I had reached the altar that lay before the temple steps and stooped down to view the inscription on the side, naming the haruspex Lucius Marcius Memor as its benefactor.

My presence was quickly noted. Already, a temple slave was hopping down the steps to intercept the new arrival waiting at the ominously dark-stained altar.

"Who—"

"Titus Laelius Calvus, of the Cult of Vitrumesh Vulcan, here to see Lucius Marcius Memor." I was proud of my chosen recipient of worship. A god of the fire-powered crafts, a purveyor of mischief, balance and destiny. A dedicated bringer of fermented concoctions from within his iconic glass chalice. A deity of ancient origins with his roots on the gritty, blistering banks of the Euphrates River in the east.

And that moment marked the first time that any other human being in existence had heard his name spoken aloud, except for perhaps the stable boy if he was in ear shot as I invented, practised and perfected its pronunciation in my room the night before.

The man blinked, but the confidence of my demeanour was

enough.

"Follow me." For the briefest moment I thought that such a simple lie was going to get me into the heart of the temple itself. The man led me towards the front steps. Those same steps lay under the gaze of a massive stone face of a gorgon. Its ugly, and surprisingly male visage (given that the gorgons were women), loomed above us atop the four columns of the temple façade.

My confidence cracked just a little at that point - it was one thing to trick a temple slave, but above me was mounted the severed head of Medusa, a monster who's eyes could turn men to stone and who's dishevelled, reptilian hair was her hairdresser's ultimate challenge. Granted, this head was just a frieze, an image carved into the stone, but it served as a poignant reminder of the ferocity of which a slighted Minerva was capable.

I mean, she didn't actually kill the beast herself, Perseus did that in a battle of demigodic proportions, but as thanks for Minerva's vague instructions about how to do the deed, he presented the head to her as one heck of a participation trophy.

With some relief, we veered off to the right towards a covered walkway that ran around the outer edge of the temple courtyard. Memor sat behind the temple itself, holding court over a large retinue of his own. Most were standing around chatting amongst themselves, so we waded through and I was presented to the man without having to wait.

"Laelius Calvus, representing the Cult of..."

"Vitrumesh Vulcan," I came to the man's rescue. Memor looked me up and down before responding.

"I've not heard of that one," he said, reaching out to a girl beside him, who put a drink into his hand. He made no move to offer me one.

"Really?" I feigned surprise. "Well, I suppose in this part of the world you wouldn't have. Vitrumesh is a vastly honoured and greatly obeyed god in Parthia, but his cult is slowly making headway further west. But surely you would have heard the story of how he battled the great serpent Oomes, drowning him in a river of beer, to bring mankind the art of fermentation?"

Memor blinked. "Do the Parthians even drink beer?"

"Anyway," I continued, "as our respective deities have similar motivations, I thought you might be interested in a united approach to reach the overlooked people of Britannia."

Memor rose, which was no mean feat, and fifteen people around him all stopped their conversations mid sentence. He stepped towards me and I prepared for his embrace...

"I'm a very busy man," he said as he walked by and his entourage fell into step behind him. I blinked as they streamed past me, then hurried to catch up, pushing my way through the crowd at a slightly faster pace than the rest as we returned to the main temple courtyard and made our way out towards the market. Shoppers stepped back deferentially as Memor passed, allowing him to move through the throng with ease. I trotted along at Memor's heels and attempted to regain my own dignity. I would need to speak a language that a haruspex would listen to.

"A serpent was slain as the priests of Vitrumesh crossed over from Gaul. Its entrails directed us here—"

"You would use serpents for haruspicy?" he asked.

"It is an animal sacred to Vitrumesh..."

"The owl is sacred to Minerva but we don't slay them for readings."

"But Minerva did not battle with owls. We slay serpents in honour of the defeat of Oomes." This conversation was not going at all as I had rehearsed but I was saved from having to rescue the situation from the brink of collapse by the appearance of a lean, verging on skeletal, man blocking our path through the market. He bowed so low he almost prostrated himself before us as he spoke.

"Haruspex Memor, a moment if you will."

Two of Memor's entourage stepped forward to intercept the man, but Memor waved them back.

"Amatus, it is good to see you, friend."

Amatus looked like he walked in social circles worlds apart from Memor's, and his manner belied Memor's use of the word 'friend' when he barely rose from his stoop.

"Haruspex, I beg of you. Zoticus still flaunts his winnings, the winnings he only receives from stealing my best cock, despite the curse. You assured me that Minerva would help, that she—"

"Take heart, Amatus. Minerva has heard you." Amatus raised his eyes, wide and moist, to look upon Memor's face with hope. "There is a boy in the town, at the corner near the laundry. Do you know of him?" Amatus gave a slight nod, his look of hope beginning to crack. "Minerva has determined that I should instruct you to purchase a generous serving of his berries and give them to Zoticus as a gift for his dinner. She will do the rest. You have the coins you need to make such a purchase?"

"But, Haruspex—"

"You would question the will of Sulis Minerva?"

"No, Haruspex, but—"

"You assumed Minerva would act entirely on her own?" Amatus did not reply. "The divine do not help those who will not act for themselves, Amatus. Now, have you the money?"

Amatus' head hung and his voice was considerably smaller than before. "I will find it, Haruspex Memor."

"Good man." Memor breezed past and continued on his way. I followed, but glanced back at Amatus. It was some moments before Amatus moved from his position, alone and dejected in the middle of the pathway.

"Tell me, priest," Memor said, and I started when I realised that he was addressing me. "Does your Vulcan work with curses?"

I blew air out of my cheeks, uncertain how to answer. "It is...

not something that Vitrumesh is commonly associated with."

"A pity. That is something that Sulis Minerva could use assistance with. There are so many."

He picked up his pace to end the conversation, but I matched his stride.

"That came as a surprise to me, I must admit," I said. "My friend Jovina described the Temple of Sulis Minerva as a place of healing, not vengeance."

That sparked his interest. He looked at me sharply and slowed down again.

"Your friend Jovina?"

"Mmm," I nodded. "She used to visit here quite regularly. She still speaks warmly of the place."

Memor studied me with interest this time. "Perhaps we can be of help to one another. Come for dinner at my house. Come by sunset. I live in the north-west district. You'll know it when you see it. Bring whatever slaves you need to attend you."

And with that, he and his entourage breezed away again, leaving me dumbfounded on the path with two problems to solve - how to find Memor's house, and the gut-wrenchingly familiar problem of how to rustle up an entourage fit for high society on a depressingly tight budget.

***

As the first stars glimmered through the skylight above, I stood in the atrium of the house of Lucius Marcius Memor. I was late, but not offensively so. Memor had been right, I did know his house when I saw it, a mansion half the size of the temple itself, but it had taken five wrong turns and six unhelpful guides before I was in the right position to see it. Now, I fidgeted with my unlaundered toga as I waited for the doorman to announce my arrival to my host.

I wished I knew why I was here.

While I waited, I admired Memor's taste in decor - simple but elegant, with a strong preference for cooler blues and greens, to enhance rather than detract from the room's centrepiece: a fountain under the skylight comprised of two human-sized, marble nymphs. One knelt to dip a palm-sized scallop shell into the water at her feet. The other stood, hunched and bearing with ease a shell of a size that I would have struggled with. She was in mid-pour; the fountain water emerged from a hidden pipe and spilled over the edge of her barnacled burden to splash down near to her counterpart. While one tipped out copious water, the other tried in vain to scoop it back up. I wondered why they couldn't just learn to share.

Their confusing behaviour was not what I found alluring. It was their blatant state of undress. Captured in marble, both women wore Greek-style chitons; dresses, which had come undone at their shoulders and left to hang, belted at the waist to prevent the garment from falling completely but leaving their torsos exposed. Flickering lanterns bestowed upon them the warm illusion of life, under-lit by reflections from the pool beneath, tinted blue and green by tiles made indistinct by the rippling water. The effect was unworldly. Their clothing swayed, their faces trembled, and, between their faces and their clothing... round and perfect and laid bare for all to see...

The pond was only narrow, if I stretched, I could touch them. I could just about...

...nearly...

...almost...

"I'm not sure your host would appreciate you getting too familiar with Doris there."

My sandal landed in the water.

There's nothing that screams 'guilt' as much as standing in a pond with a semi-naked statue. As I shook my foot of excess drips, I glanced back to glower at the source of my surprise, hoping to pass my flushed cheeks off as anger. The newcomer giggled.

I could not stay mad at her.

A young woman stood near the door. She was slender and small of stature, fair skinned and now etched in my mind as the source of inspiration for at least one of the nymphs.

"Doris?" I asked.

She pulled herself into a relaxed but upright pose, and recited with a slight over-pronunciation of her words. "'To Nereus and to Doris of the lovely hair, daughter of Oceanus, the completely encircling river—'"

"'—there were born in the barren sea, daughters, greatly beautiful, even among goddesses.'"

Her mouth made an adorable little 'o' shape as I finished the quotation. "You have read Hesiod?" she asked.

"Hesiod, Homer, and anyone else my father thought worthy of study. Cato the Censor was in there too, but he was much less lyrical."

There was that giggle again, and my knees wavered underneath me. I returned my gaze to Doris; the daughter of a titan and the wife of a god. She was more than just a nymph, she was an Oceanid and the mother of fifty water spirits known as the Nereides. Tiber and Enica had nothing on Doris' parenting capabilities.

"She's my mother, you know." The woman appeared at my shoulder and looked up at the statue's face.

"Doris?"

Hades, that giggle; I stood no chance against it.

"No, of course not," she continued. "But my mother posed for the sculptor. At least her face. I don't know about her body, that might be someone else. But either way, I don't think the upright and pious Lucius Marcius Memor would take too kindly to you groping her."

My face flushed as someone cleared his voice behind us. We turned to see an older man whose under-bite gave him the impression of a permanently annoyed canine.

"Gallio!" said the woman. She skipped towards him. "I've just been telling our guest about Doris. He's read Hesiod, you know?"

He dipped his head to her. "The Master has requested your companionship."

"Of course."

My eyes followed her as she left the room, before I looked back at the slave. I couldn't be certain if he had heard her comment, but I had a fair idea. I offered some pleasant words of introduction. He responded with no more than a curt nod and a 'follow me.'

***

"Can we get on with this?"

The woman, introduced to me merely as Marcella, had flopped down onto the middle of the oversized dining couches. I have to say, that despite the plushness, vibrancy, structural integrity and societal conformity of Memor's furniture, the decor lacked the character that my own Lounge of Uncertainty would have imparted.

I lay on the third of Memor's couches - the one traditionally reserved for the least important guest. Upon my entry into the dining room, Memor had taken my tardiness graciously, stating that he was pleased for the chance of an intimate dinner between us.

An intimate dinner had a different definition to Memor than it did to myself. I had brought a slave to see to my every whim - a stable boy called Expectatus, on loan from the owner of my

61

accommodation, who had taken to the challenge of providing me with an adequate waiter with relish.

With relish, and a horse brush.

Memor and Marcella had taken a different tack. They were each equipped with a slave for their every whim. One to pour their drinks, one to pass them plates of food, one with a supply of napkins on hand to swap out for the used ones after every third wipe... ultimately, the dining room had every appearance of a theatre restricted to standing room only.

I would guess that neither of them would have any qualms about undressing in Sulis Minerva's changing room.

"Now, now," Memor calmed her. He popped a blackberry into his mouth as he spoke. "All in good time. Calvus here has been telling me today about a cult of which he is a member. An epithet of Vulcan, I believe?"

I waved Expectatus forward to serve me from a selection of spiced prawn balls and an asparagus omelette but he didn't move a muscle. I tried to pass off the movement as a stretch as they watched.

Marcella giggled.

"Vitrumesh is more than just an epithet," I explained, my voice a little hoarse and I struggled to clear it. "Many Romans would equate him with Vulcan, and indeed they are similar. We use his name with Vitrumesh's for introductory purposes only. But Vitrumesh is very much his own deity, with a distinct form of worship."

"Oh, how so?" Memor asked. Marcella suppressed a yawn, but as I glanced at her, she winked at me and I felt the corners of my mouth curl upwards.

"Well, Vulcan is a god of fire," I explained as I returned my attention to her uncle. "Vitrumesh is a god of fire and water. He uses both to create. For example, when heated stones are placed within liquid malt, it creates a beer of such sweetness that it is unique, a gift from the gods." I nodded towards the glass bowls on the table in front of us, containing our pre-dinner delicacies. "You yourself benefit from Vitrumesh's talents, Marcius Memor. Sand, soda and limestone, when heated within an intense fire, combine to create a liquid of such viscosity that it can be moulded and crafted by artisans, but it is only in the presence of continual heat that these creations are successfully solidified into the glassware that adorns your table tonight. The dichotomy brings divinity."

Memor raised the glass from which he had been drinking up to his face, a clear glass tumbler, painted with such skill as to challenge even the best of Tiber's work.

"Fascinating," he said. "And you said that it was your friend, Jovina, who suggested that you bring your cult here, to Sulis Minerva for help?"

I stole a look at Marcella. Her eyes were downcast, and my chest tightened.

"Well, not in so many words. My neighbour" – and I stressed the word 'neighbour' – "described the temple here and I made the connection myself."

"You're an astute man."

"It seems to be a natural alliance, really. Vitrumesh uses water to create, Sulis Minerva uses water to heal."

Memor nodded, returning his gaze momentarily to his glass before taking a sip. "There may be some truth to that. What do you need to get started?"

My heart pounded just a little faster than before. "Well, we're starting from scratch here. We need a place to set up. I was thinking about Londinium for that, I understand that Aquae Sulis is Minerva's territory and I don't want to encroach on that. In fact, I saw you in Londinium, at the Temple of Mars and the Imperial Cult."

He grunted in affirmation as he drained what remained of his drink and passed it back to a waiting slave. "Petronax has established a nice base for himself there, under my guidance. And you would be wanting something similar for yourself, I take it?"

My eyebrows shot up in spite of myself. "Something like that, yes."

"Well," Memor paused to think. "I would imagine that a god such as Vitrumesh would need access to a creek or a stream, or the river itself. With ease of access to additional fuel? For fires?" I nodded, no longer trusting my voice. "Then you may be in luck. I do own a parcel of land in Londinium. Up behind the amphitheatre, alongside the creek. Would something like that suffice?"

My arms and legs tingled. I cleared my throat. "I'd need to inspect, but yes, that sounds promising."

Hades. Without quite knowing how, I had won the support of the Temple of Sulis Minerva and secured the land upon which to build my temple. Part of me started to think that maybe Vitrumesh was real, and he was guiding me to make this stand for him.

Of course, if he was real, the divinely ordained talent for glass working had yet to make an appearance in me, but maybe he wanted me for my suave business skills instead.

"Of course," said Memor, "we need to work out a way that you can help Sulis Minerva in return.".

"Advertising," I suggested, without skipping a beat. There was no other practical or physical asset that I could offer otherwise. "The Temple of Vitrumesh will be a selling point for the power of water, and the power to heal, directing those who come to us in need to make the expedition to Aquae Sulis."

"That's not really what we need right now," said Memor. "We are quite well known."

Marcella snorted but Memor threw her a look and she

dipped her head in apology.

"Forgive Marcella, Calvus," Memor continued. "She has a lot on her mind and she's not herself. You see, her cousin has gone missing."

"Oh, I'm sorry—"

"I think Minerva has led you to us."

"Um...how so?"

"Well, some time ago, Marcella cursed the person who abducted poor, young Vilbia. You said that Vitrumesh does not work with curses, but I think you could help us. Specifically, because of who you know."

"May he who carried off Vilbia from me become as liquid as water," said Marcella, her face twisting into a grimace as she spoke, spitting out the words. "May she who obscenely devoured her become dumb, whether Velvinna, Exsupereus, Verianus, Severinus, Augustalis, Comitianus, Catus, Minianus, Germanilla or Jovina."

"Jovina?"

"Tell us of this Jovina of yours, priest," said Memor.

"Ah..." I glanced from Memor to Marcella. Having said her piece reciting the curse, her form had crumpled. She was weeping. Softly and without noise, but her eyes were moist and she dabbed at them with her napkin. Memor followed my gaze and reached across to grip her hand.

"Pet, if this is too difficult for you, you may retire. I'll have dinner sent up to you."

She nodded. "Yes, yes I think I ought." Without thinking, I arose from my couch to help her but she waved away any assistance. "Thank you, but I'll be all right. It was lovely to meet you, Calvus. Keep reading Hesiod, won't you?"

And with that, she glided from the room with a troop of personal waiters in tow.

***

I sank back onto my couch and returned my attention to Memor. He looked at me with a steady gaze.

"Now you see how you could help us," he said. "We've ruled out a few suspects over the years, but we're no closer to finding Vilbia. You said your Jovina was familiar with the temple here. If she is the same Jovina, your help would justify the Temple of Sulis Minerva to provide you with the land that you seek."

"I... I don't know where to begin."

"Then let's fill you in." He signalled for more wine and Expectatus finally leapt into action, watching the movements of Memor's trained sommelier and mimicking him as best he could. He filled my glass so full that any sudden movement spelled disaster.

"You see," Memor continued. "Marcella is an orphan. I'll cut to the chase but you need to know. There was an illness spreading amongst the family. Young Vilbia was the first to be stricken. She was a small thing, not much more than a baby. Marcella doted over her and, with no siblings of her own, her young cousin was as good as a sister.

"It was heart wrenching. Weeks of fever and coughing, the poor little creature, hardly able to breathe. Her parents - Marcella's uncle Gaius and his wife, implored upon Minerva to help. Vilbia was given waters from the spring to drink and they waited and hoped.

"Minerva was merciful. The child was spared. But, the goddess' price was high. Gaius, his wife, then Marcella's parents Lucius and Marcia, were in turn struck down and withered away, and this time Minerva could not be swayed."

Memor paused for a moment as he bowed his head. I glanced at the door through which Marcella had retreated and thought about the face on the statue outside. It commanded pride of place; the first impression any visitor had of the house proper - the mother of fifty in place of the mother of one. It made sense for a temple official to honour the gods in his household, but what must that be like for Marcella, to walk past her mother's face each day, set in stone?

"It was a sorry situation, and what else could any man do but to take the two girls, Marcella and Vilbia, into his care? I took both girls into my house. I bought a nursemaid, and the girls grew up together under her care. They were very close, as you saw in Marcella just now. Vilbia is slightly younger than Marcella. She would be approaching fifteen today, while Marcella is seventeen. How old are you, Calvus?"

"Twenty-one."

"Then, you are young enough to remember life at the age of the two girls - carefree, trusting, thinking themselves immortal."

He was hazarding a guess at my upbringing - carefree was certainly not amongst them, locked away with my tutor.

Immortal... well, I still wasn't sure that I wasn't.

The conversation paused while the mains were brought out.

Poached chicken, a stuffed hare, and side dishes of beans, nettle patina, and spicy mushy peas. The first course taken away, merely moved over to make space for the additional dishes. With the quantity of food on offer, I wondered if Memor had been expecting other guests to arrive and had been stood up.

"Tell me, Calvus," said Memor. "When you were growing up, did you ever think about running away from home?"

I chuckled. "All the time."

"Forgive my intrusion, but might I ask why?"

"Boredom, I guess? My father had an annoying habit of wanting me to do well in life. That clashed with my schedule."

"But I bet as you grew older, you came to realise that he had your best interests at heart?"

"Ahh..." I shrugged and grinned.

Memor smiled. "I think that you and Vilbia would have been friends. As she got older, she never really saw eye-to-eye with me. I wasn't her father, after all. But, I did my best. Look around you, this is not a house in which family members go wanting."

I looked down at my food, slopped onto my plate with the aid of Expectatus' training in the equine culinary arts, but as I finally got to taste the food prepared, it was revealed to be exquisite. The poached chicken was served with a sweet dipping sauce, flavoured with mint and date (and a small amount of the mustard sauce from the beans, but I put that interesting combination down to the server, not the chef).

"The tipping point came two years ago, when Vilbia overheard me discussing their situation with a colleague, whose son was a potential marital match for Marcella as she neared womanhood." He paused, and for a moment the confident façade of the haruspex dropped as he winced and cleared his throat. "She misunderstood the gist of our conversation."

"Misunderstood what?" I asked.

He prodded at his food with a finger for a moment before continuing, gathering his own thoughts.

"She thought that I blamed her for the deaths of their family. The sickness began with her, but she could not be to blame. The gods are fickle beings and we must keep them appeased. The cost of appeasement for Minerva's help was high.

"So, Vilbia ran away. One morning, the nursemaid went to rouse her and she was gone. We don't know whose idea it was, whether Vilbia decided on her own accord or was goaded by another, but we do know that she had help. The shutters on her window were broken, she wouldn't have the strength for that."

He looked vaguely ill. I did a quick check on the table for red berries, but there were none.

"It's the not knowing," he said. "She could have walked back through the door at any time, but..."

I sighed, glanced at my food and then back at Memor. "Why do you suspect Jovina?"

"Jovina, the Jovina in the curse, was a go-between for the baths and the temple, a low level priestess who worked in healing. She got along well with the girls, but she had... misguided concerns about their upbringing, being without their mothers."

"But would she have really taken her?" The Jovina I knew would have avoided the extra hassle at all costs, but Memor was lost in his memories.

"Urgh, that screech..." He grimaced, then seemed to realise where he was and shook his head. "Perhaps. She was quite, ah, vocal in her concerns."

That figured.

"What of the other suspects?" I asked.

"Some have been ruled out. Others, well... let's just say that I have other opponents who would wish me ill. But, that is not for you to worry about. Many are no longer an issue, and your only focus needs to be Jovina."

I thought for a moment, but he was wrong about that.

"Marcella mentioned an Augustalis in that list. Jovina herself was recently widowed, not that she's mourning. Her lover is a brute called Augustalis."

"Augustalis is with Jovina?" he asked, his face ashen as his eyes darted back and forth in thought. "Sounds like she might be the one. What do you say, Calvus? Can you help us find Vilbia and finally return her to her loving family?"

Would I help?

Would I help to reunite a confused child with her bereaved family, potentially rescuing her out of the dank pit of a house that Jovina thought adequately met the needs of her offspring, while simultaneously securing the land I needed to set myself up for life?

Absolutely.

"I'll help."

We got stuck into our meals and the subsequent conversation that night between myself and Memor continued onto frivolous topics and temple administration.

"Out of interest," I asked, "what do you charge for curses?"

"Half the value of the missing item."

I could only guess how much richer the temple had become on the back of the curse for a missing family member.

7

I was a man on a mission. A chap with a challenge. A priest with a puzzle.

If I were to find Vilbia and win the land I needed for the temple, I needed to speak to the people who knew Jovina. The next morning I headed to the bathhouse, made use of my week-long pass, undressed and went in search of her former colleagues.

Laelius Calvus: the nude investigator.

A wax tablet for note-taking is of no use in a steamy bathhouse, but it turned out I didn't need it. When I tried to speak to the staff, they were either too busy, too coy, or too recently arrived to be of much help. But there was one person I knew I could trust to be frank and honest with me.

I found Varro-with-the-gimpy-leg openly pissing into an access point of the water pipe, in a utility room between the spring and the bathhouse. I was pretty sure that this section of the structure was strictly staff-only for maintenance reasons.

"You'll get yourself barred if they catch you doing that," I greeted.

"They haven't yet." He looked back over his shoulder at me, the stream strong and ongoing. "You got over your phobia of undressing in front of gormless idiots?"

"They did me the courtesy of blinking occasionally to give me moments of privacy."

"If you want more time than that, just say you saw me tossing a signet ring into the hot pool. They'll panic and go running. No-one wants me breaching their security perimeter and stealing their master's stuff. They'll leave you in peace for a while while they search." He shook himself off and turned to face me.

"Thanks for the tip." I said. "You've been here a while,

right?"

"About twenty minutes now. Particularly large drinking session last night."

"No, no. I mean, you've been coming to the baths for a while. Years? I need your help to solve a mystery."

"Ha! What are you, an informer now?"

"Actually, yes," I puffed my chest out and grinned. "I'm on a case."

Varro-with-the-gimpy-leg's cackle sounded like a rusty sword scraped against his ancient, disused shield. "A glass-blower, some sorta religious nut, and now an informer? You change roles faster than I change loincloths."

"You can add beer brewer to that list, but yes, I guess I do. This is a one-off thing, though. For blatant personal self-advancement."

"You workin' for that lot, or against them?" He nodded in the general direction of the temple.

"Which answer will get you to help me?"

"Ha! Go on, then. What do you need to know?"

"Did you ever meet a woman called Jovina working here?"

"Oh," his eyebrows shot up. "Is that who you're trying to find? That case, I'll definitely help you. A nicer woman you would never meet."

"Pardon?"

"Pleasant to talk to, brilliant at what she did. About the only one here that would tolerate me."

Something clicked in my mind. "Oh, you mean for prostitution."

"What? Of course not. She was chaste, kind and loving. Don't know what happened to her though. Just disappeared one day."

I shook my head. I thanked him for his time, wished him well on his quest to annoy a goddess, and left.

Back in the changing room, I considered using Varro's stolen ring ploy to gain some much desired privacy as I prepared to dress and leave, but I wasn't given the chance. As I opened my mouth to speak and start the vicious rumour, with my towel wrapped tightly around my waist, I was interrupted by a voice behind me.

"Laelius Calvus! One last visit before you head home?"

There stood Memor, as naked as the day he was born, and apparently none-the-wiser to the way his gut hung over his crotch like some sort of fleshy veil. Maintaining eye contact was a challenge. I tried to pass off my downward drifting eyes as part of a nod.

"Haruspex. Quite. It's... it's an experience, that's for sure."

"The things Minerva provides for us," he said, "are a blessing indeed. Her restorative waters will put you in good stead for your tasks ahead."

I wondered if I should warn him of the additives that Varro-with-the-gimpy-leg had provided for her 'restorative waters', but there seemed to be no tactful way to broach the topic. Perhaps the yellow waters had yet to enter the bathhouse proper. Perhaps he was merely pissing in an outlet pipe, taking spent water away to the river. Who was I to assume otherwise?

Maybe it was too late anyway - Memor's skin, when viewed this closely, did already have a certain gorse-yellow hue to it.

The debate in my mind of whether or not to warn him had left me standing with my mouth open to respond. As no words had yet formed, all I could do was to close it again in silence. Memor's eyes narrowed as he regarded me.

"When do you intend to return to Londinium?" he asked.

"Just as soon as I gather up my belongings from where I am

staying."

Memor waved away that idea. "Nonsense. Stay another day. I have been called to Londinium on an urgent matter. I leave in the morning. Travel with me. Tell me more of this Vitrumesh of yours."

I had run out of Vitrumesh stories to tell but I imagined that Memor travelled in greater comfort than if camping on the roadside.

"Thank you, I would appreciate that."

***

Memor told me where to meet up with his retinue the next morning.

He didn't tell me who we would be travelling with.

North of town, he had marshalled together five covered wagons and a small army of bodyguards. That was travelling done right. The troop had been told to expect me and I walked up the length of the wagons, wondering which was mine.

They were glorious:

Enclosed spaces contained a bounty of cushions and blankets, to travel in temperature-controlled comfort.

Heavy curtains across the door ensured privacy.

Arched wooden roofs kept the rain off.

Four wheels were mounted on a metal and leather suspension system for never-before-experienced (at least by me) smoothness.

Bright colours and a range of mounted medallions bearing the head of the Medusa and Minerva's owl adorned the outside for divine protection and style.

Bliss.

Honestly, the plaustrum at the back would have been fine. A flat-bed goods transport laden with all the baggage. I could have made do using a trunk as a stool and it had four wheels, which was four wheels more than I had had on the way over.

As I neared the front, the curtain of the second wagon was pushed aside and out stepped Marcella. My heart stopped. She looked at me and giggled.

"There's my Hesiod-reader," she said.

"Mar—Marcella."

"Don't look so surprised. Didn't Uncle Lucius tell you? I'm coming to Londinium, too."

"Uncle Lucius?"

"Memor. He and my mother were siblings."

In my mind, the face of the Doris statue superimposed itself onto the body of the haruspex that I had had the misfortune to witness yesterday. That was something that was impossible to unsee.

"Brother and sister?" I asked. "Adopted?"

"What an odd question to ask." Her brow furrowed as she regarded me and I wished I could start the conversation over again.

"Ah, Calvus, you're here." Memor appeared at my shoulder and I blushed. I think that Marcella knew where my mind had gone in that instant. If not then, then at least when she saw my eyes involuntarily move to his gut.

"Marcella will be joining us," Memor continued, none-the-wiser about my mental image. "I hope that is acceptable—"

"Of course," I was a little too quick to answer. The corner of Marcella's mouth flicked upward.

"Now," he continued, "where is your mount for the journey?"

"Oh, um..." I looked wistfully at the carriages before gesturing to where I had left Marcus and Tractus tethered to a tree nearby. They were busy butting each other, fighting over what was left of the tuft of grass between them.

"Oh no, no, no, no," Memor exclaimed. "That will never do. Take them down to the baggage handlers. Yes" – Memor looked me up and down – "I think Pedasos will be a good match for you."

Memor had overestimated my horse-handling abilities. Pedasos was a sprightly, slender and tall piebald stallion, equipped with fine leather tack and bronze and silver trappings bearing ornate swirl patterns polished to the nth degree. He was a proud beast fit for the senatorial class, and he took my measure in a matter of seconds. The more I tried to heave myself onto his back, the more he spun around in a circle away from me. I hopped alongside, locked in an unimpressive, one-leg exercise routine. Memor's groom watched on, trying not to laugh.

"Perhaps Stultus would be more to your... style," he suggested, and waved forward a shorter, heavy-set grey, bearing basic equipment only.

Stultus was more my style - he froze while I hauled myself up.

He also lingered when I tried to kick him into action, loitered as the convoy moved off, and waited around as the last of Memor's party passed me on the road.

"Stop that," the groom called out as he passed me kicking and rocking in my saddle like a madman. "You're confusing him. Just squeeze once with your knees, relax, and let him go."

I calmed down. I tried as he suggested. Stultus took his first hesitant steps, but not before releasing a low, long fart.

I missed Marcus.

***

Riding upon Stultus involved forming an uneasy truce but we made it work. An hour down the road, after a considerable "getting to know you" session in which I learnt to trust him and he learnt to tolerate me, he consented to me pulling alongside

Marcella's carriage window. She drew back the curtain and grinned at me.

"I don't think that's quite the mount that Uncle Lucius had in mind for you."

I dipped my head. "Pedasos is a noble beast, well trained and a credit to your uncle. I thought my skills would best be of use training Stultus here to match his stablemate's bearing and skill."

She giggled. "Uncle Lucius passes Pedasos off to all new members of his entourage. It's his little game. No-one's mounted him first try yet."

"Oh, thank Minerva for that!" My whole body slumped with relief. "New entourage member?"

"Uncle Lucius likes you, Calvus. I think he's taken you under his wing. Look out, here he comes."

I rode a little straighter and ducked my head as Memor slowed his horse down to draw alongside us, hoping to hide my rather chuffed expression from the man himself.

"Haruspex. Not riding in your carriage?" I asked.

"Not yet. We'll see how long the healing waters of the bathhouse continue to work on my knees, though." He glanced down at Stultus. "Everything okay?"

"Quite. I was just talking with Marcella, to ask why she was making such a long journey."

Marcella smiled. "Well—"

"Marcella is going to become the model of womanhood for Aquae Sulis," said Memor. A flicker of annoyance passed over her face but she let him continue. He smiled at her. "She will be dedicating an altar in Aquae Sulis to worship the Emperor's Virtue."

"The Emperor's what?"

"Virtue."

I looked at Marcella and she explained. "When worshipping

the deified Emperors, us provincials find it hard to consider all aspects of their epic personalities in one go. It's too much for our feeble, little mortal minds to take in, so it is common in the provinces to find altars dedicated to just one small part of it. Personally, with an ego that size, I'd find it hard to haul the weight of it out of bed each morning."

"Marcella!" Memor snapped as I snorted. "I'm hoping this journey will do you some good."

"Well," she threw him a look of protest. "They're just men. Dead men—"

"Respect, child, that's what you need. That's what you'll learn. If not in Londinium, then onwards to Camulodunum, to the heart of the Cult of the Deified Emperors in Britannia." Memor looked at me and a hint of pride returned to his posture. "She is to become a municipal priestess."

My eyebrows shot up. "A priestess! That's quite an honour."

"It means I get to nursemaid for the image of the Empress, keeping the dust off it and occasionally lighting a candle on special occasions. I don't get to do the fun stuff, like Uncle Lucius here. Slice open still-beating hearts—"

"It's no less important," he admonished. She rolled her eyes. "I think spending some time talking to Laelius Calvus here would do you the world of good, Marcella," Memor said. "He knows the importance of duty."

"Ah… duty?" I asked.

"Yes, duty to your family. Duty to your gods."

Duty to my family was best left unmentioned at this point. Duty to the gods - well, I had invented my own, but that didn't mean I thought of the rest as unimportant. They knew how to throw lightning bolts.

"I believe we need to do as the gods request of us."

He nodded. "Good. Because Minerva has need of you, Titus," he said, switching over to use my first name, normally reserved for family and close friends. I let it lie, but however our relationship was developing, I was under no impression that I should start calling him 'Lucius'.

He continued. "Minerva needs you to fulfil your duty here. This is about more than just a missing child. This is about Minerva's reputation, her very strengths. She will guide you on your way, but you must not fail. To do so would signal to the world that she is incapable of looking after no more serious a threat than a stolen bath towel, like so many of the curses she receives through the Temple. This is her big test, to show to the people of Britannia that she is a great and powerful goddess. To show the people that Rome brings her biggest strengths to help the common folk. Minerva and Rome will be humiliated if you fail, Titus. Now, if you will excuse me, I need to check on the others."

He pulled on his reins and his horse fell back to the carriage behind us. I sat in the saddle, feeling the pallor in my cheeks and jaw agog, until I swallowed.

"So, no pressure then."

Marcella giggled.

8

Travelling with Memor was worlds apart from travelling equipped with a one-man tent. Had I been the type to write a travel journal, my description of the route to Aquae Sulis would have been:

Disappointed by the onset of existential crisis sleeping under the stars. Also, no toilet facilities.

The way home was more:

Pleasant conversation, safety in numbers, and roadside guest houses with complimentary towels in the bathhouse. Ten out of ten, would do again.

As Haruspex, Memor was entitled to, and could afford to, stay at the imperial mansiones that dotted the route every thirty miles or so. These guest houses were for weary, wealthy travellers and were far more up-market than any stable I had ever hunkered down in, with individual rooms, mosaic floors and doors that closed the whole way.

On the second evening, I stepped out onto a patio overlooking rolling hills and flat fields. I supposed the point was to watch the sunset, sipping wine from actual glassware - a sign of superiority in the world of short-stay accommodation, which had no doubt factored breakages into the cost of the stay - and to think romantic thoughts of Sol's commute through the crimson skies.

The only thoughts coming into my head were about where I might find a blanket. I started as Marcella's voice sounded behind me.

"Titus. Come and join me."

She had claimed a cluster of lounges and lay propped up on an elbow with a light woollen shawl draped over her legs. Her toes poked out the other end, tinged pink in the chill, but she didn't seem to notice. With a drink in one hand, she gestured with the other to a bowl of olives sitting on the table nearby. I sank into the lounge opposite and popped one in my mouth.

"Why are you mad with me?"

I swallowed. Largely unchewed, I felt every moment of the olive's journey to my stomach, pit and all. "Mad?"

"You've barely spoken a word to me since we left Aquae Sulis. I can't help but wonder why." She swirled the drink as she spoke. Warmed wine, presumably well watered as was decorous, but so heavily spiced that the aroma of fennel and peppercorns reached my nose as it arose in the steam. I wasn't mad with her, far from it. My silence owed itself to the knot that had twisted up my stomach ever since her uncle's speech about duty and the humiliation of Rome.

Her eyes followed mine to her drink and she regarded it with curiosity.

"I've always wondered how they do that," she said.

"Do what?"

"The pictures." The glass she held was crude but the blowers had at least tried. Left with its natural yellow hue, the tapering vessel was drizzled with strands of glass to form a wonky diamond pattern: the pride and joy of some enthusiastic beginner. A beginner who, afraid of the fire, had worked at arms' length from the heat.

My chance had arrived - my chance to wow her with something real about me. Me, who had slithered into her noble life on the basis of a deception and statue-groping dubiousness.

"That's nothing special," I said. "My business partner and I run a shop on the west side of town, atop a steep hill overlooking the confluence of two rivers and accompanied by the percussion of a water mill and a chorus of ducks and moorhens."

And a little too close to a tannery when a westerly wind blew, but let's not spoil the imagery. Too much reality always spoils the imagery.

I described our venture in all its sweaty rainbow glory and the elaborate results of Tiber's hard work. Her eyes widened.

"Glass is shaped by the actual breath of its creator?" Her voice hinted at amazement, awe even. "You give it the air from your own being to bring it forth? And you do all that as part of your priesthood?"

"Uh, of course."

"Amazing," she murmured, looking at the glass anew and letting her eyes wander from it and off into the sunset. We sat in companionable silence until she turned to face me again.

"So, why are you ignoring me?" she asked.

I sighed. "I'm not. And I wasn't. It's just... well, your uncle."

"He hasn't told you not to speak to me, has he?"

"No, it's not that."

"Ah." A look of understanding fell over her face. "His 'good of Rome' speech?"

I nodded.

"Just ignore him. He's always going off like that." She pulled her chin in and deepened her voice in a fair imitation of Memor. "'We are the spiritual elite, Marcella. We must ensure obedience. That is the road to wealth.'"

I gave half a grin but I didn't feel any better about the situation. I looked at her face and her green eyes looked back at me so earnestly that it made me feel worse, so I looked away again.

"What... what if I screw it up?" I whispered. It was going to be my name scratched in lead at the bottom of the spring by the end of the month. Maybe they'd go easy on me. Maybe they'd just ask Minerva something like, 'may he always sit down on a wet bench when wearing a clean tunic.'

I don't think I owned a clean tunic.

Marcella regarded me.

"Look, Titus" – I glanced at her – "do you have family?"

"Um. Yes. In Rome."

"But not here?"

"No. We had a falling out."

There was that all-too-familiar look. The "what on earth could Calvus have done" look.

"Over your dedication to the Cult of... I'm sorry, I knew it, but it's slipped from my mind."

"Vitrumesh." I chuckled. "No, not over that."

She nodded. "That's almost a shame. It takes courage to adopt the gods of distant lands, to spread their name."

"You know, that's the nicest guess anyone's ever made about why I moved to Britannia. Normally people assume it has something to do with public nudity or acting."

"We're all actors, Titus. No shame in that. And we're not all as fanatical as my beloved uncle. He pulls that speech out on anyone who can do something he wants. He's got way too much practice at it. But the glory of Rome is not what I want." She paused, considering her next words. "Is there anyone in your family that you miss? That you would like to see again?"

"Yeah, my youngest sister. Tertia."

"Tell me about her."

And I did. I told her all about the time we had conspired to make our older sisters believe there were ghosts in the house. I told her about balancing along water holding tanks and, when she inevitably slipped and sliced up her knee, how she hid the injury from our parents so that I wouldn't get in trouble. And I told her about the time she told my first crush that I had fought off at least ten gladiators to protect the life of a puppy, just so that I might get my first kiss. My first crush wasn't that naive and the honour of my first kiss had to wait for someone else, but the thought was there.

By the time I was done, we were both in hysterics.

"She sounds wonderful," said Marcella.

"Yeah, I miss her."

She dipped her head. "She sounds a bit like Vilbia. I miss her too." She sat back in her seat and I had to lean over to see her clearly. "That's why I know you will look for her, Titus. Don't worry about Uncle Lucius and his duty speech. Find her for me."

9

In the days that followed, I had time to come up with a plan. It was brilliantly masterful in its simplicity.

I would break into Jovina's house and look for clues.

I was an informer now, with a client. That gave me license to do whatever I needed to in order to find answers.

Definitely.

Without a doubt.

So, why in Hades did it make me feel so guilty to be lying on my stomach atop the boulder that separated our houses, shielded by the branches of the walnut, being shat upon by wood pigeons, and peering at my neighbour's house until such time as I saw her leave?

I was not fortunate enough to have struck them on a day full of errands out of the house. Smoke pushed its way out of the chimney as a baby cried, breaking the predawn stillness. It would be just my luck if today of all days was to be a lazy one at home for Jovina and her family.

Time dragged. Hours after the sun had risen, Pacatus put in an appearance to throw scraps out to the chickens, reaching into a bucket with his slender arms and scattering handfuls of unidentified muck across the yard – treasures for the hens to discover. At least someone was attempting to clean up in there. The scraps were sparse and too far gone for human consumption, no matter how desperate. The chickens didn't care. They fell upon them the instant they hit the ground.

Perched up on my rock as I was, I needed entertainment. A fowl battle over food. There was no 'one cuts, the other chooses' solution to poultry breakfast-time disputes.

I waited for it to begin, for Coquam to assert her dominance over her smaller counterpart with a squawky warcry declaring herself queen of the compost.

And I waited...

...

And waited.

Chickens are too polite. Where was the blood? Where were the savage pecks to the head? There was a reason they didn't put flocks of hens into the arena. With three sisters and myself at the table growing up, dinner time was a race to the finish. To the victor: an overstuffed stomach and an evil sense of glee at having deprived the others of what was fairly theirs, despite the best efforts of our housekeeper-turned-peace-keeper.

Hades, this was boring! Day one back in Londinium, and I was already pinning hopes on the appearance of a wayward maggot to keep things interesting. Laelius Calvus: the nude investigator was more fun than Laelius Calvus: the frozen investigator, in the mid-autumn morn.

Late morning rolled around and while I was lying on my back tossing a pebble up into the air and catching it (I was on a winning streak of twenty-six before it inevitably smashed into my cheek), Jovina at last left, with a baby strapped to the front of her body, another to her back, and Pac maintaining a safe distance of three feet behind. They picked their way up the road and disappeared into the forest. I swung into action with the speed of a cheetah.

An aged cheetah who had been squished into a rock crevice since the crack of dawn.

I slid down feet first. The rock surface formed a natural file against my soft belly and ruined a serviceable tunic. Damn Jovina. I felt justified in blaming her as I hobbled towards her house. If she wasn't a suspect in a case, I'd never have been up there in the first place. I vaulted over the gate to prove to myself that the stiffness in my muscles had everything to do with the discomforts of a long surveillance and nothing at all to do with the early onset of age. I made it over, too. I would have performed a neat little flourish upon landing for the entertainment of the chickens, but for the crick in my back, and as a result, the hens were not impressed. Pluma fled. Coquam glared at me and stood her ground.

The door would not budge. Whatever Jovina's faults, she was at least consistent when it came to security, and I was left with only one option before shoulder-barging the door in the vain hope that the frame was more rotten than it appeared.

I tried my own house key.

It turns out that the original builders of our houses used the same locksmith, and that locksmith was lazy. I pushed the key into the lock, slid the latch open with ease and slunk in, closing the door behind me.

Jovina hadn't bothered to clean since my last visit. There stood Minerva on her pedestal against the far wall, shiny and pristine, surrounded by the Lares bearing aloft their cornucopia. I turned them all around to face the wall - perhaps it was they who had granted me access, but I didn't want to chance it in case they resumed their role of protecting the house against intruders - and I got to work.

Nothing promising turned up.

A desiccated apple in a cupboard.

A copper ring behind the latrine bucket.

A damp rag growing mildew in the corner behind the dining table.

The living area revealed nothing more than the signs of a person who was the antithesis of a clean-freak.

The two bedrooms were no more revealing. Jovina occupied one with the two babes, Pac took up the other. Both were much as you'd expect for a single mother with toddlers and an older son. The floor of Jovina's room existed somewhere under the toys, clothes and blankets. Pac's room was sparse and had a hastily installed, crooked latch on the inside of the door, for a boy at an age when privacy was a key issue and forethought was not. It had been broken several times and re-nailed to the wall. Who knew what he had been doing when his parents had presumably busted in on him. If it was anything like what I got up to at that age, then shame on him.

With typical apathy on his part, the window shutters in his room were left to bash around in the breeze while the family was out. So much for security.

I went back outside and ignored the sour taste forming in my mouth.

Jovina couldn't be the cleansing, aquatic healer that Memor sought. It was a case of mistaken identity after all. Technically, she hadn't even said that she had been to the Temple of Sulis Minerva. As Memor had pointed out, 'we are quite well known'. Her description might have been from hearing about it, not seeing it - second-hand information passed on by an acquaintance, or a friend.

Marcella's happy reunion and Memor's promise of land were already slipping from my fingers.

As I pondered the next step, I felt a nibble at my toes. Pluma squatted at my feet, picking off some bugs that had wandered onto my boots. She was gentle, timid and kind, her ruffled feathers betraying her status as the bullied one of the pair. I could almost like chickens if they were all like Pluma - meek and easily harangued. But where was her oppressor? My eyes drifted around the yard, riddled with dandelions and dead seed heads, until I spotted her scratching around for caterpillars by the shed door.

The shed.

I could have kicked myself. Of course, if Jovina kept anything incriminating around, she wouldn't keep it in the house where the babies would use it as a makeshift toy for teething. It would be separate, away from prying eyes such as mine.

I picked my way down the path and inspected the door. It was locked, and my luck had run out - this time my key would not work. I didn't know the first thing about picking locks.

But, I knew someone who did.

***

Pheidippides was the person most on my mind as I ran the distance from Jovina's house on the far west of town, past where the newly-arrived Tarraconensis Troupe were building their temporary performance stage, and hooking a right at the Forum to reach the city docks in the centre.

He was not on my mind because he was the person I was running to see; he was on my mind because he was the runner who ran from Marathon to Athens, six hundred years before my time. He had been sent to announce to the Athenians the news of their victory in battle over the invading Persians. Having burst through the door, pronounced the word 'nikomen' - we won - to the gathered crowd, he then promptly dropped dead on the floor.

Apparently, the distance between Marathon and Athens is a little further than the distance from Jovina's house to the centre of town. However, I think I deserve the same amount of credit for completing my epic test of endurance.

And when I burst through my actual quarry's door, the word I pronounced before sinking to the floor was a little more profane than 'nikomen.'

My quarry didn't care. He barely even acknowledged me except to say, "you just missed him."

"What?"

89

Dio, merchant-extraordinaire and the source of the cullet that Tiber and I used to create our glass masterpieces, was busy adjusting the weights and measures of his set of shop scales. He was not in the least concerned that I might expire in the doorway of his warehouse. If that were to happen, he had a perfectly handy dinghy moored across the road that could be utilised to dispose of the body; it probably wouldn't be the first time, to be honest.

"Tiber's just left," he said. "We've sorted out the old cullet issue, came up with a solution that solved problems for both of us. You can tell him that he can expect his delivery first thing in the morning."

"That's... that's not what I'm here about," I managed to get out between heaves. "I need your lock picking skills."

He looked sharply at me.

"What lock picking skills?"

I looked to my left. A large, military-style trunk lay nearby, its barrel-shaped padlock open on the floor.

"Oh, come on," I said. Dio ran a profitable import/export business running whatever clients needed between Londinium and Gaul. Rarely did he ask what those items were. Sometimes, his profits came from honest trade. Sometimes, they came from siphoning off things that would not be missed.

He grunted. "Fine. It'll cost you. Where's the box?"

"It's a shed, back at my place."

It turns out Dio knew a bigger range of profane words than I did.

***

Dio was a stocky cube of a man, whose body was longer than his legs. I put that down as the cause of our slower pace back to Jovina's. When we made it back, I was relieved to note that there was no sign of Jovina. No screeches, no crying children. The hens were still scratching around in the yard as before.

Laelius Calvus: the lucky investigator.

Dio noticed the care with which I looked around as we approached the shed.

"This isn't your shed, is it?"

I bit my lip. "How much for you to not ask any more questions?"

"Another denarius."

Greedy sod. I dipped my fingers into the pouch at my side and passed him a silver coin. He took it and gave his full attention to the lock with a low whistle.

"Tricky one they've got here."

"But you can crack it?"

He took a moment to inspect it but he nodded. "Yep."

He pulled out his tools and got to work. Armed with a collection of bent prongs and narrow pokers, he felt the need to explain things as he worked.

"They've gone up-market on this one. Most door locks, you see, just need a key with prongs that fit into the holes on the inside of the bolt, to hook in and pull it across. Damned easy to pick, those ones. This one's a tumbler lock, you've got to lift the pins inside the lock to be able to pull the bolt across. Need the right shaped key to get around the wards inside... are you listening to this?"

I snorted.

"No."

Dio looked up at me. "I'm telling you this for a reason. I'm not doing this for you again, next time you're on your own."

"What? Why? You can name your price."

"Then let me ask which customer I'm losing."

"Not going to happen." I was adamant about keeping my motives to myself, especially when Dio was involved. I'd have to explain about Jovina and then he'd want to get involved and claim a cut of my land from Memor, and then the conversation would just get awkward. I wouldn't put it past him to go behind my back, find Vilbia himself and claim my rightful reward as his own.

"Then you're on your own," he said.

He looked back at what he was doing and something gave underneath his fingers.

"Got it," he said as the door swung open. "Let's see what we've got." While breaking into neighbourhood sheds might not be a wise business decision, it went against everything in Dio's nature to crack a lock and then not have a good sticky-beak inside.

The shed did not house what I had expected. There were no hoes, no pitchforks or sickles. Shallow shelves, three high, lined the walls and bore an assortment of instruments I would not have picked as gardening tools; their arrangement as pedantic as it was possible to get. On one shelf, knives and saws were laid out with such precision that I half expected to find their silhouette in paint upon the shelf to ensure their correct replacement after use. A collection of long-handled spoons rested on the shelf below, arranged by size.

But, perhaps their owner was not as careful as it appeared at first glance. Gaps existed where tools had not been returned, although whether lost, loaned or broken I couldn't hazard a guess.

Three crates sat on the floor, two of which were nailed shut and one lay open and empty bar the remnants of packing straw and coarse cloth wraps, yellowed with age.

Dio picked up a small knife with a leaf-shaped blade and wooden handle and tested the point on the tip of his thumb. I picked up an L-shaped pair of tweezers, hinged on the long side. As I squeezed them together, the short side opened to the width of about two fingers.

"A medical person, huh?" he asked.

"A temple healer, I've been told."

"Because you know what that's for, don't you?" he asked, nodding towards the tweezers in my hand. I glanced at him. "Rectal speculum," he explained. "That's what they use for looking inside you."

To my credit, I didn't drop them. But I tried to hold them by no more than my fingernails as I gingerly placed them back on the shelf.

"So, not for gardening?"

"That'd be an unusual way to manure your cabbages."

I knelt to inspect the crates. Of all the tools laid out around us, nothing looked suitable to prize open the lids. They were dusty. But, there was something. Something small, which had fallen between the boxes. I strained to reach between them, my fingers brushing against and then closing upon my prize, and it was at that moment that we were discovered.

"What are you doing?"

I yanked my arm free, earning a number of splinters for my efforts.

"Pac..." I turned to face him in the doorway. To my relief, he seemed to be alone. "Your mum's not with you, is she?"

"Why?" he asked, as he took a step backwards from us.

"Well, I'm out of here," Dio said. "Nice to meet you, kid. Everything's on him." He jerked a thumb in my direction as he sidestepped around Pac. He looked back at me as he departed. "Tiber. Delivery tomorrow. Don't forget."

I looked at Jovina's eldest. His eyes were wandering around the shed, with a hint of confusion. "Pac, we need to talk about your mum."

His gaze flicked back to me with an expression that implied he was ready to turn and run after the departing Dio. I didn't wait for his objection.

"Have you ever met a girl called Vilbia?" I asked and his face paled.

"Who?"

"I met her uncle the other day. They're trying to find her, her uncle and her cousin. They need to speak to someone called Jovina. I didn't think it was possible that your mother was the same Jovina, until I saw this." I turned to look back at the contents of the shed, and when I turned back to Pac, he had gone.

"Pac!" I ran to catch up with him on the path as he hurried towards their house. I stopped him as he fumbled with his key in the door lock, already puffing after such a short sprint.

"Get out of the way!"

"They're distraught, they need their family together again. If your mum knows her, or has any idea—"

"You have no idea!" he shouted as he turned to face me, his eyes brimming with tears. "No-one does. She doesn't want to be found."

"You do know where she is?"

"No. No-one knew, not even Eratosthenes, not until..." he renewed his efforts to get through the door.

"Eratosthenes? Not until what?" A question occurred to me that I should have thought to ask long before now, had I been in any way interested. "Just how did Eratosthenes die, Pac?"

"It doesn't matter. Leave us alone!"

He abandoned his efforts at the door and took off down the path. I didn't try to follow, it was no use. Instead, I regarded the small item I clasped in my fingers: my prize from between the crates.

It was a small doll, a figurine of a girl with her arms crossed, not unlike some of the toys chewed upon by Tiber's kids on any given day. But just why was this one hidden away in storage and not a source of relief for Jovina's twins as they cut their own little incisors?

10

Laelius Calvus: the lucky investigator had morphed again. Now, I was Laelius Calvus: the let-slip-to-the-son-of-a-potential-murderess-that-you're-stalking-her investigator.

These by-lines were getting less poetic as I went along. What a fine informer I was turning out to be. Working at the temple, alongside physicians and priests, who knew what skills Jovina had picked up with a fine blade over the years? Skills involving highly sensitive parts of the anatomy.

I heard it that evening as I sat down to a hearty meal of next-to-nothing. When one spends the better part of two weeks travelling to a luxurious spa town on the other side of the province, then gets back and spends the intervening time spying on the neighbours, it leaves very little time for grocery shopping. That night's sole offering from the pantry basket on my bench was a carrot that could bend tip to top without snapping. It was accompanied on my plate by an egg that I had appropriated from Jovina's hen house before departing the scene of the crime earlier that afternoon.

The noise that heralded the end of my feast was not the usual cacophony of homicidal indigestion from Jovina's at meal time. It had more of the ring of actual homicide to it, and it was getting louder as she approached my house. I had my doubts that she had missed the egg. This was about something much worse. I took the opportunity to barricade the door and douse the lamps while Jovina squirmed her way through the rocky outcrop between us.

"Calvus!" I heard her key enter the lock, her key that would open my door as well as hers, but the door did not give way with the expected ease that she had anticipated - it banged hard up against the Lounge of Uncertainty, which did me proud by holding firm against the attack.

"Calvus? Calvus, I know you're in there! What in Hades is this?"

A clatter of something hit the door. Something small, and perhaps metallic. I could only picture it as being items from the shed.

"A man's dead and you take the opportunity to start looting? Or did you know? Did you know what was there?"

More futile shoulder barges against the door.

"You're complete filth, Calvus!"

The couch gave half an inch before its legs stuck fast on a raised floorboard and her willpower faded. I dared not move for ten minutes after she had left, and that was a good thing. Not long after the assault on the front door had abated then came the thunk thunk of more eggs arriving at my house, but these ones not as fresh as the one I had for my dinner.

I hoped Memor's appreciation for my work would stretch to providing a house cleaner once all this was done.

***

I was in over my head.

Have you ever lain in bed at night wondering how someone might be killed with a rectal probe? I have. I'll bet Jovina has as well. Just how wide do those things open up? Were they sharp? Could they be used to deliver some sort of poisonous deposit, to be sucked up into your body backwards, defying all sense of logic, reason and dignity?

Had Eratosthenes found out the answers to these questions the hard way? The more I thought on it, the more colourful the mode of his death became, and the more deft she became with her instruments. I left my door barricaded overnight. That morning, I squished my way out of the narrow bedroom window. After a rough night's sleep, I had resolved to retreat to the workshop to gather my thoughts.

There was one problem.

After my departure, I was not sure where Tiber fell on the 'likelihood to murder Calvus' scale. I suspected about a seven. Maybe a six-and-a-half; he had had a fortnight to get over the personal injustice done to him, after all.

Perhaps Fortuna, the goddess of good fortune and luck, would help me out as a favour to her half-sister, Minerva. Or her full-sister, Doris. No-one was quite sure who Fortuna's father was, but of the two prime suspects, Jupiter and Oceanus, both had other offspring with a vested interest in this case. Surely they'd enlist Fortuna's help on my behalf and she would gift me with the luck that I needed. I'd arrive at the shop and Nux would be swinging his legs on the stool, left alone in charge, while Tiber was out on a vital, and lengthy, errand.

When I arrived at the shop, I leant on the front door and the hinges creaked. Tiber was in my face in an instant. Sod Fortuna and her lack of sisterly love. I winced, waiting for the blow to strike. This was it for me - not death by rectal probe, but death by blow pipe. Perhaps a more dignified end, unless Tiber was in a creative mood.

"Great, you're back. Come and see," he said and I cracked my eyelids open to peek up at his face. He was positively beaming.

"What, no 'where have you been?' No 'about time?'" I asked.

With the merest lowering of his brow and dipping of his chin, Tiber's happy, beaming face morphed into an evil grin. Perhaps death was still an option.

"You left me running this place alone," he said. "You're not the only one who can have big ideas. Difference is, mine will probably work."

"Tiber, what have you done?"

"Come and see."

He led me into the storeroom. Everything seemed much as before. Tools on the left. Finished works on the right, crates of cullet in the middle. Except...

I shrugged. "I don't know. You've got a new storage frame?"

The middle was looking a little more organised. New amphorae sat propped up, holding the materials ready to be worked. As we watched, Nux hauled in another and wrangled it next to the rest. He looked glum. I suppose we could have helped him, it just didn't occur to us.

"We've had a delivery," explained Tiber.

"Oh, right, that. Dio said. Well, good, I suppose." Replenishing our supplies was neither a big decision, nor what I was there for. "Look, Tiber—"

"Oh no, wait," said Nux. "You haven't heard the best part of this yet."

"Glass, Calvus," Tiber continued. "Proper, Britannic glass. That's what we'll be making."

"We already do that."

"Not like this. We take the waste from Gaul, whatever over-worked scraps they see fit to throw our way. But this... this will be local. Our own."

I felt my brow furrow and I glanced at Nux. He wasn't just glum, he was morose. His eyes were fiery and his jaw jutted. But no witty comebacks. That in itself wasn't a concern - I was fair game for his smart-arse comments, but this was Tiber. Nux was normally content to go along with Tiber's ideas, excited even. But not this time.

"Just what is in those amphorae, Tiber?"

"Have a look and see."

I hesitated, then sidled up to the stand. One was already cracked open, ready for inspection. Inside was not the hodgepodged mix of broken glass shards I had come to expect from Dio. I reached in to pulled up a handful of the contents, and let the fine white power filter through my fingers.

"What is this?"

"Our future, Calvus. Forget about that religion of yours. This is how you grow. Honest work, quality products."

I stared at him and Nux guessed the question that was struggling to come out of my mouth.

"It's salt," he explained. I baulked at the quantity.

"Salt? Just how much money did Dio trick you out of?"

Tiber pouted. "It's not salt," he grumbled. "It's soda. All the way from the Alexandrian delta, the best source in the Empire. The Syrian masters rely on this stuff."

"Who told you that? And rely on it for what?" I knew the answer to the second question, but I was just so hoping to hear something else, for some other idea emerge from Tiber's lips.

"Dio, and for glass making of course. Raw glass, from scratch. With no more reliance on imported cullet."

Damn.

"Think about it, Calvus. We'd be the only ones. We won't just be working glass, we'll be making it. We can supply raw glass to blowers throughout the province, or else keep producing our own goods and market it as genuine Britannic glassware."

"Are you nuts?" I asked. "The work involved..."

Tiber had described raw glass making to me once. We'd have to dig the sand, and the lime... melt it all down at much higher temperatures than we could do at the moment. Nux would never sleep again, manning the furnaces. Tiber was strong but getting on in age, which would leave me to do all the digging. I could see my life of tedium flashing before my eyes. That was not what Titus Laelius Calvus was born to do.

But then I remembered that my life may be measured in days at this point.

"I... whatever. I don't have time for this. I have a murder to solve."

"A what? Who's been murdered?"

"Eratosthenes. Probably."

"Probably?"

"Well, possibly. Maybe."

I brought Tiber up to date of what had transpired since my glorious departure astride Marcus ('asinine departure, more like,' Nux chipped in, looking profoundly chuffed with his pun).

"So, let's get this straight," said Tiber. "You met a man in Aquae Sulis who's lost his niece, and that's evidence to you that a clerk in Londinium was murdered by his wife?"

"The same wife who might have a hand in the disappearance of the niece, and keeps tools in her shed for looking up people's arse holes. Maybe Eratosthenes fought with her, maybe he tried to help Vilbia and she knocked him off to protect herself. Why would Pac be so evasive?"

"He's what, eleven? Twelve? Go figure. And all of this is at the behest of a priest who may have ulterior motives behind his concern?"

I resisted the urge to growl in frustration. "I'm going to get to the bottom of this."

"I'm sure you're going to try, and I can't talk you out of it, can I?"

I spun on my heel and marched towards the door. "I need to speak to Memor about all of this."

Tiber called out to my retreating back as I left the room. "Just don't make a bad situation worse by mucking about when you don't understand."

***

Sod what Tiber thought. Memor was right. His Jovina and

my Jovina were one and the same, and the promised land was within my grasp. I wove my way to the mansio within which Memor and Marcella were staying.

Let's just say that Memor travels in style. I knew that already - the pilfered linen at home on my bed vouched for that aspect of his personality, a souvenir from our journey together. But on the road eastward, the only options available had been the equidistant government travel lodges or a tent. Here, in Londinium, there was a tyranny of choice. Memor had made that choice well - he had picked a mansio south of the river, close-at-hand to the Procurator's residence and a stone's throw from the Temple of Mars Camulus and the Imperial Cult. It was one in which the in-house sommeliers knew the difference between Falernian and Calenian, decantered under a flawless sky and never, ever served pre-watered.

I would never get away with a B.Y.O stable-boy waiter here. There was a hopeful part of me that thought I might be invited to dinner and yet a logical part of me that really hoped that I wasn't. Nux might almost, *almost*, be able to handle the situation but the first irresistibly snide, backhand remark would see us both out on our ears.

A doorman, who stood head and shoulders above me and several tree trunks wider, asked... no, told me to wait in the courtyard while he announced my arrival to the guests. I didn't argue. Call me perceptive, but his gallant and deferential manner was not the reason this man guarded the door. The only reason I was allowed in at all was because he had my name on a list. The courtyard was spacious and filled with superlatives and marketing adjectives to impress discriminating clientele. They could have tossed cushions on the daybeds; instead, they were 'positioned'. The evergreen topiary wasn't pruned, it was 'manicured'; the decor was 'artisanal' and the adjourning rooms bore 'bespoke' mosaic designs in black, red and white.

I guess, technically, every mosaic is 'bespoke' given the manner of its construction. In a period of profound tedium, the mosaicists lay one thumbnail-sized tessera after another thumbnail-sized tessera until they've covered a dining room floor the size of my house. They charge as if it's hard, but all they do is follow the coloured dots on a plan. Glass-blowers face years of practice and the first drunken rage sees their work smashed and gone forever.

Maybe I could take my frustration out on the whole pompous situation by pilfering a cushion to go with the linen on my bed. They looked pretty shiny, and shiny fabric meant more upmarket than I could afford. But, shoving a cushion up my tunic might have been a sudden weight-gain that even the doorman would be a little too sceptical to believe.

As the autumnal breeze made an entrance over the rooftop, I was summoned from behind by a voice that made my legs melt.

"Titus! What a surprise!"

There she stood, draped in a loose blue shawl that floated from her arms. The doorman hovered behind her, shoulder-to-shoulder with Marcella's own private lady's maid, but Marcella was having none of it.

"I'm sure you have somewhere to be?" she asked of him and, with a departing glare in my direction, he bowed and left. The lady's maid remained, but she might as well have been a statue as far as Marcella's notice of her went. I didn't mind, as it meant her full attention was now upon me.

"Are you here to see Uncle Lucius?"

"I... ah..."

"Titus, I'm so sorry," Marcella cooed. "He's left already. I'm afraid you may have had a wasted trip."

"Left?"

"He said something about meetings and business, and nothing I should worry my little head over." She rolled her eyes.

"Really, he still thinks I'm six."

"I'm sure he's just looking out for you," I said.

She grinned, stepped up beside me and hooked her arm in mine. Her lady's maid's face flushed on her behalf. I know mine probably did as well; my ears had ceased to feel the chill.

"Come on," she said, steering me towards the entrance. "You can help me show him just how much I have grown up."

"Um..."

"We're going shopping."

11

"Marcella, I don't think this is the time—"
"Nonsense," she said. "It's always time for shopping." She steered me towards the door and out onto the street. I glanced at the doorman as we passed, half hoping he would prevent the situation and half hoping that he wouldn't, given that his way of 'preventing the situation' would probably result in some form of bodily injury for myself. From his expression, it was clear what he thought, but he did not interfere.

"Let's walk," she said, as if she honestly expected me to have a litter of my own parked just around the corner. "I want to see the city, I want to explore."

"But it might not be safe. Jovina... I found something."

She stopped and looked at me.

"What did you find?"

"I really should talk to your uncle about this."

"Bah!" She spun on her heal and kept walking. "You're all alike."

"Marcella, it might not be safe."

"Why not?"

"Because if Jovina did what she did to Vilbia, she might try it with you as well."

"No, she won't."

"How can you seem so sure?"

"Do you think you could abduct the niece of Haruspex Lucius Marcius Memor off the streets of Londinium and get away with it?"

I glanced back towards the mansio, afraid that that was how

this would appear should Memor arrive home to find Marcella gone.

"It's happened before. Vilbia is his niece too."

"No, she isn't."

"What do you mean?"

"Vilbia isn't Uncle Lucius' niece. Uncle Lucius is my mother's brother. Vilbia is my cousin from my father's side."

"Oh. But does that distinction really matter?"

"Of course it does. Now, where's the best place to go shopping around here?"

I pointed towards the bridge back across the river. There was one place in Londinium to take the pampered niece of a wealthy man with an urge to spend.

The Forum.

The Forum was exciting because it was new. Well, not new, new. Londinium had had a Forum about as long as Londinium existed but I'm told it was made of wood. Wood. That was never going to scream imperial glory to anyone.

Imperial rustic, perhaps.

Don't get me wrong. 'Rustic' is good. 'Rustic' is honourable. 'Rustic' is what the elite think they are being when they vacation at their acreages, watching their four hundred slaves tend their wheat fields and olive groves. But 'rustic' was never going to win over a recalcitrant, unimpressed province.

Urban splendour was what this situation called for.

Urban splendour was radically different from anything Britannia had seen before. The province had experienced military might. The province had seen religious magnificence, in the form of the Temple of Sulis Minerva and the fabled Temple of Claudius at Camulodunum. Both of these brought the element of fear - the divinely-supported power of a culture that was here to stay, like it or lump it.

Fear subdues. Fear does not win hearts.

Opening up the province to the world of new and amazing creature comforts is what wins hearts and for that, a mega-market was required.

The Forum stood three floors high, four wings of business offices and bankers' vaults - now in use but still encased in construction scaffolding as the long-awaited finishing touches were added. These four wings bounded an inner courtyard, which hosted a market that brought forth all the wonders of the Empire, carted up from the docks on a daily basis. Hispanic olive oil. Egyptian papyrus and Anatolian marble. All items that Britannia had never had before, and never would have if not for the Romans.

Life is short. You could spend it planning uprisings that will make it even shorter, or you could spend it trying on new clothes.

Which would you choose?

"Ooh," Marcella made her choice as she swathed herself from a bolt of fabric. "What do you think?"

"It looks nice."

"Nice? Do you know what this is?"

What a silly question. It was obvious what it was.

"It's blue."

"Blue?"

"Slate blue."

The look she threw me was withering, but the next words I heard did not come from her.

"It's Serican silk, from lands far beyond the Empire."

Those words came from the man behind the trestle table, his eyes twinkling. It should have been a look of pity directed at me, but he knew me too well. Dio grinned.

"The lady knows quality. Come on, Calvus, how much will you be purchasing?"

When Dio is relaxed, his natural facial expression is a slight lopsided smile and a fixed gaze that implies that he can see into the depths of your entire being, and what he sees there he both accepts and finds amusing. That would be a good quality in a friend - no matter how ridiculous he finds you, he would be there to help you. But, in a merchant, you can't help but worry that he has foreseen everything you could be about to say and is already three steps ahead of you.

That is not a good place to be in while haggling. Besides, I hadn't forgiven him for the soda sale.

"Come on, Marcella, we can find better elsewhere." I tried to guide her by the elbow away from the stall, but she was having none of it.

"No."

"I'm sorry?"

"How much?" she asked Dio.

"More than he can afford."

"I don't think it would suit him."

They haggled until Marcella waved forward her lady's maid with the purse and Dio set to work cutting off a significant length of fabric. He folded it with a deftness that was at odds with the chubbiness of his fingers, received a thanks from Marcella, and then she was off down the way.

We passed piles of tanned hides and charcoal, stopped at stores offering candles and woven grass baskets, and navigated walkways through the scaffolding and sections roped off with 'exciting new shops coming soon!' signs. All the while not a word or a look passed between us.

I had to break the silence.

"I'm... sorry?"

"Good."

Birds twittered and bees buzzed, or at least the busy marketplace equivalent thereof, in the form of consumers haggling and slaves hauling, and silence resumed between us.

"What am I sorry for?" I asked.

She stopped and looked at me.

"Don't tell me what I can and can't buy."

"I didn't mean—"

"Nobody tells me that I can't have something I want."

I didn't know what to say to that, so we wandered on as she passed over fine red Samian pottery on account of concealed scuffs on the base, and sampled the difference between forest and heather honey.

A drawn out buzzing sound drew our attention to the eastern entrance, as first one, then two, then an obnoxious number of tibia-players pushed their way into the crowd and formed some sort of honour guard, blowing into their double-fluted instruments to create a crescendo of discordance. To my ears, and no doubt to most others if they had any sort of musical taste, it sounded as if swarms of bees were panicking, encased inside and incensed by the continual flow of air from the musicians' mouths; air scented with last night's onion-heavy feast.

Braving the honour guard came forth acrobats, jugglers and dancers, twirling and dancing and generally showing off.

"You going to the show?" asked the honey-seller.

"Show?" asked Marcella.

"Heard they're in town for the month. A Hispanic troop. Threw together a theatre for themselves over near the fort. Starting with a pantomime, I hear. Good for a night out."

I glanced at Marcella and she inferred what I was thinking.

"Oh, gods no," she said. I blinked.

"Really? I would have thought—"

"Pantomime? Titus, really? How old do you think I am?"

"Fair point. What else do they have on?" I asked the man.

He shrugged and I passed over a few coins for a pouch of honey-roasted almonds. Children clapped and mothers laughed as their acrobats flopped and flailed ever closer to us, until they were upon us in all their brightly-ribboned glory.

Blue streamers flicked across my face as a tibia-player blasted noise at me, as if having the piercing sound a hairsbreadth from my ear would make it any more bearable. More of the company appeared around and between us as Marcella was forced backwards, her head intermittently bobbing over the crowd as she strained to find me.

Discomfort was an incentive to these people - the more they prized me away from Marcella, the greater the grimace on my face, the more they took it as a challenge. They were worse than children.

Children...

I mimicked the most capable father that I knew of, when his children were acting up for attention. Tiber would just ignore them. He would avert his eyes, experience the onset of sudden deafness, and walk away. So, that's what I did. I spun on my heel and strode the other direction. I didn't run, I didn't dodge their antics, but walked and browsed and examined goods on offer until they got bored with me and left.

The only problem was, I now had no idea where Marcella was, and in a busy marketplace as large as this I would be unlikely to just bump into her. But, on the off-chance that I would, I was going to be prepared.

I ducked back to Dio's stall. He looked at me, then shouted towards the fruiterer in the stall beside him.

"Hey Maccalus, you owe me a denarius."

"Not yet I don't," came the reply. "He ain't told you what's happened yet."

I looked at Dio, who grinned back at me.

"I bet him you'd be cast off before the day is out. Maccalus gave you the benefit of the doubt because he's a big softie at heart, aren't you, Mac?"

"Young love, ne'er bet against it."

"And yet, here he is, with no girl on his arm—"

"I'll take the hairpin," I said, gesturing to a carved oak piece with flared ends.

"Ha!" Maccalus cried out in triumph but Dio didn't budge.

"And how will you be paying for such a piece? Fine craftsmanship, brought down from the north at great peril—"

"In that military chest that miraculously fell open in your warehouse?" I asked with an innocent expression.

Dio's smile wavered and we haggled a price that seemed fair.

"I think she's used to a little more than just old driftwood," Dio said as he handed the piece over.

"I think you underestimate her graciousness."

I found Marcella in the most sensible place in the world, perched on the edge of the fountain that took pride of place within the market. A central, eye-catching landmark that would draw all lost souls towards it.

"My lady," I said, performing a quaint bow. She turned towards me and giggled. "We have to stop meeting in fountains like this."

She raised an eyebrow. "Promise me you won't grope this one."

I glanced up at the lithe form of Mercury, god of shopkeepers and merchants. There was little chance of that.

"Just tell me this one isn't modelled on your father." My heart broke at the pained look she threw me and she turned. I gripped her elbow. "No, don't. I'm sorry. You and your uncle both have gone through too much to have to listen to crass jokes like that."

"Thank you. And, sorry, I shouldn't be so sensitive. It's just, well... those actors."

I rolled my eyes. "Yeah, my ears will be ringing to the beat of 'fingernails on a slate' for a week."

"It's more that they bring back bad memories for me," she said. "My uncle, my father's brother, Gaius. He married a mime actress. He wasn't known for making sensible choices in life."

I could understand her concern. Actresses were considered little better than prostitutes. For someone as noble as a member of Marcella's family, marrying one would have been scandalous at best.

"I suppose I should thank Uncle Gaius, though," she continued. "It's because of his choices that my father met my mother."

"What do you mean?"

"My father tried to convince Uncle Gaius against his plans, but it was no use. 'Love', Uncle Gaius called it. But then Papa heard that a new man had arrived at Minerva's Temple, a man who seemed to have the personal ear of the gods themselves. His skills were beyond compare, he could fix anything, adversity just vanished into the breeze. It is little wonder that a person so blessed becomes a spokesman for the gods.

"Papa prevailed upon him for help. Perhaps this Lucius Marcius Memor could do what Papa could not and convince Uncle Gaius of the futility of his plans but if not, if he would not be swayed, then perhaps this Memor could call upon Sulis Minerva to cure the woman who was my aunt, to have the sacred waters heal the spiritual illness inside, to wash away any cravenness that existed within her and so that she could become a respected member of the family."

"Through meeting Marcius Memor, who brought his sister along, my father met my mother, and well..." she shrugged, the rest obvious.

"And did Sulis Minerva come to their assistance? Did she help your aunt?"

"I suppose she did. For several years, my aunt and uncle remained childless. I was born, and yet, they still had no progeny.

My uncle did not divorce her, he said he would rather have no heirs than lose that woman. But finally, when I was three, Vilbia was born. It had taken time, but it seemed Uncle Lucius' pleas on their behalf were heeded. The family was peaceful. For a time."

She drifted into silence and there was not much I could say in response to her story, so I didn't try. I was developing a history of saying the wrong thing to mourning women. It was safer to avoid the issue. I reached into my pouch and pulled out the hairpin.

"I bought you this. I know it's a poor value compared to—"

"Oh, Titus, it's lovely," Marcella said as she took the pin from my hands. She held it for a moment as she looked at me.

"I'll bring you much better next time, glassware—"

"Of all the colours of the rainbow?" she asked, as she passed the pin to her lady's maid for safekeeping.

I chuckled. "That might be a challenge, but all right. Now, I really do need to see you back to the mansio before your uncle returns, otherwise he'll be after my blood."

She threw me a half-grin. "All right, then. But only because the clouds are getting darker and I don't want to be caught in the rain."

12

My next plan was just to confront Jovina.

Why not? With Memor unavailable and Tiber unconvinced, I'd have to go it alone.

But not on an empty stomach. This was going to take strength and the sum total of food I had eaten in the last thirty hours was a carrot, an egg and enough honey-roasted almonds to fit in the palm of my hand. I stopped along the way at a takeaway for a concoction involving pigs, chickens and snails. I resolved that should I survive this, I would take a keener interest in my food and find out what the little round seeds were, floating in the mix - they were fun to crunch on.

The plan was to meet her on my terms, reveal all I knew about her and force her to confide in me where Vilbia was hidden, through sheer weight of argument.

The plan was to get out of there before she demonstrated her medical skills and terminated my life in the way experienced by Eratosthenes.

The plan did not go according to plan.

Don't worry, I did make it out of there with all parts of my posterior still attached and functioning as well as they ever did. In fact, my bowels may have even been a little looser than normal. The fact was, though, that I never got to speak with Jovina at all.

When one goes to confront a potentially homicidal, child-stealing maniac, one must go armed. That should go without saying, but I didn't have so much as a paddle with me. Thankfully, I had just the thing under my kitchen bench at home.

It was a wooden spoon the size of Priapus' phallus, a rural deity whose endowment was so large it entered the room several seconds before he himself did. Something that size as genitalia apparently presented the little god with a number of inconveniences, but when in the form of a spoon, it made brewing a large batch of beer a breeze.

Once I had the spoon in my hand, I would be in control of the situation, or I could at least keep Jovina at bay by wielding it as a spear. But Jovina had shown herself to have a mean throwing arm, and access to a ready supply of sharp instruments. I thought about that as I headed home and squeezed between the boulders that divided our houses and released the breath that I didn't realise I was holding as I had crept past her front fence. I would need some form of shield, which could be...

...my front door, apparently.

It hadn't just blown open. It had been kicked in so hard it had come off its hinges. Granted, such an act would take no great strength, given the woodworm, but surely that level of response to my questioning of Pac was a tad over-dramatic?

I stepped over it with some trepidation and was confronted with what I thought was the worst of the disaster first.

The Lounge of Uncertainty.

My precious dining couch that conformed to the curves of my body and took me to paradise each time I lay on it, lay in ruins on the floor. Left against the doorway when I had vacated the house that morning, it had borne the full brunt of the force that broke through the door. Tipped up and on its side, two legs had splintered clean away. To add insult to injury, the perpetrator of the crime had kicked the frame further into the room, scraping its polished side through the dirt. My vision focused in on that for some moments, all else around me just blackness of the walls of the tunnel. But gradually, that blackness faded, the colour of the room slowly returning around me.

And that colour was a dark, syrupy brown.

"No," I muttered, as I stumbled over upended stools to look

behind my kitchen bench. "No, no, no, no."

My amphorae of beer, and all my glasses, lay smashed upon the floor.

She knew. Jovina knew what I was doing, and she was coming for me.

And there was one thing that made matters even worse.

My spoon was gone.

***

Hades!

As I stared at the brown liquid glimmering on the floor, and mourned the drinking sessions it would no longer see, I thought of my strongbox.

My strongbox is a matter of perception, really. I had pilfered it from a way station somewhere outside of the port of Narbo, while en route to Londinium. The staff assumed that a small box, tucked into the bottom of a crockery cupboard in the common room, empty and forgotten, would not be the target of a petty thief. They thought wrong.

It is strong. It's made of wood, with little reinforced bronze corners. But there's no lock and it's not heavy. It's only about the size of my boot - a toddler could march in here and waddle away with it without a second's thought and so, as the vessel into which I poured my wealth, it needed to be kept hidden.

Well hidden.

In a place where no thief, experienced or otherwise, would think to look.

But in a two-room shack with a faulty front door, that was always going to be difficult, so I relied instead upon the balance of effort versus reward. In a house such as this, a thief would not expect glorious riches to be at hand and would be forced to weigh up the value of dragging the bed frame across the floor to

116

reveal the loose floorboard under which the box lay.

I hurried into my bedroom, relieved that the furniture inside remained largely as I had left it, if a little dishevelled. It gave me cause for hope because, honestly, the rumpled blankets on the bed and the upturned basket that served as an approximate target for dirty laundry looked much as they did on any other day. The teeth-splintering screech as I dragged the bed across wooden floor added discomfort to hassle as part of my thief-proofing measures.

Once that dentally-debilitating deterrent had been overcome, the floorboard under which I had hidden the box was revealed, and I brought forth my treasure, still intact.

With the thousand denarii that I had stashed within accounted for, I spent some time digging the hole under the floor a little deeper and replaced the box, now camouflaged under a layer of dirt, back into its hidey-hole. But not before I had removed the other item from within its confines - the small doll that I had found within Jovina's shed.

Then, I tried to do something that does not come naturally to me. I lowered myself onto the edge of the bed and thought rationally, turning the doll over in my fingers.

Outside, it started to rain. A few drops turn into a shower, which turned into a barrage. Rain always gave me some level of anxiety - that goose-pimply, stomach-twisting anticipation of structural leaks, slumps or warps - but, for the moment, the drenching downpour and treacherous puddles offered security against return visitors.

I must say, rational thought has its benefits. Irrational thought is much more fun, but rational thought has its place. What did I know, and what were my options?

I knew I lived next door to a maniac.

I knew that there was no turning back from this. What would I do? Go up to Jovina, and say, 'hey, I know you probably killed your husband and that there's a missing girl who's life is very much in danger, but I promise to keep this all between ourselves if you promise not to kill me'?

No. I had to see this through, I had no choice. So, my only option was to find Vilbia, find out what happened to Eratosthenes, and then pass the whole problem over to Memor to sort out. He would know what to do, and I would be free of Jovina and safe to build my temple on his land. That was the best outcome for everybody.

Except for Jovina. And Pacatus and the babies. But, Pac was old enough to take on responsibility now and they'd be safe.

Unless Pac was in on it.

I ran my hands through my hair. Urgh. What a mess.

Okay, so...

I needed evidence, either of Vilbia's whereabouts or Eratosthenes' murder. There were no clues to be found in Jovina's house and shed as to Vilbia's whereabouts, so it was to Eratosthenes' murder that I had to shift my attention to next.

Just what makes compelling evidence of a murder?

A body, definitely.

A plausible motive.

An eyewitness to the event.

A bloody knife, or a frying pan with the victim's facial features imprinted into the base.

I was forced to admit that I had none of those things. The body was gone. Tiber had heard my reasoning for Jovina's motive and had dismissed it out of hand. If Pac had witnessed the event, then he was certainly not coming forward to tell us all about it. And, as for the murder weapon...

The shed housed plenty of contenders but the problem was, from what I had seen, they were all impeccably clean.

And I could not stay here.

I grabbed a sack and crammed it with clean-ish clothes and a blanket. It was only a small sack so I had to be choosy. That wasn't hard. It's not like I'm spoiled for choice when it comes to finding socially acceptable apparel. I propped the door back up against the frame and headed to the workshop, destined for Nux's sleeping pallet as my centre of operations until this was over.

***

The rain had abated, which meant only one thing. Jovina could now ambush me on the path.

I had no choice. I would have to follow the river's edge and sneak around the back of her house. Once past our little river flat, I could climb up and rejoin the road to town. I could have walked south, away from her house and towards the Tamesis, but I knew the banks were steeper and prone to flash flooding. So, I headed north, which took me on a route directly behind Jovina's house but promised gentle floodplains and an easy amble back into town.

With my sack slung over my shoulder, I squelched through my yard down to the river, keeping low and slow along the bank.

Laelius Calvus: the stealthy investigator? No. The nude investigator was still my favourite. A steamy bathhouse with the possibility of a massage suited my style more-so than a saturated river's edge with the possibility of a murderous end. I could see her house looming above me, up on the rise, the sinister single story cottage with shuttered windows, daisies, and a little path leading down to the river for fetching water.

I wondered if that was where it had happened, where Eratosthenes had died...

I shook that thought out of my head. There was no point dwelling on the ease with which Jovina could have pushed his body into the water and watched it drift away to become

119

somebody else's problem. Nor was there any point in dwelling on just how many lampreys' stomachs were now filled with the meat of—

I pressed on past the house and around the embankment that defined the northern edge of habitable flat. Above me was rocky scree and forest. The path I trod was narrow, a mere foot wide between water and levee, which made for slow going.

Of course, the river north promised to deliver expansive flood plain, and it did – on the opposite bank. On my side, the river nymphs were not so kind. As I made my way north, the water's course took a sweeping bend to the left, cutting into the riverbank as it did so, and leaving in its wake a steep, slick, eroded bank that flaunted the shiny skid marks of defeat each time I attempted to scramble up. I was left with no choice but to keep rock-hopping my way north in the hope that the river, and my luck, would turn.

I am not made for rock hopping along river banks. I'm made for beer-drinking sessions and honey pastries when I can get my hands on them. My sticky, sticky hands. Rock-hopping requires a certain level of core strength that I simply do not possess. The worst of it came when my foot slipped between two rocks, into what appeared to be a shallow puddle. Looks are deceptive. One leg stayed on the bank, the other went straight down to my mid-thigh, leaving me doing some sort of v-shaped split that required flexibility beyond my ability and providing the opportunity to practice some of Dio's profanity while I extricated myself.

Around the bend, the ground finally levelled out and I emerged into an open, blissfully flat woodland that welcomed me with wild flowers, bee-stings and poison ivy.

I'm not really a nature person.

To my right the woodland continued, somewhere beyond which lay the route to civilisation and public toilet facilities. To my left lay wasteland, or close enough to it, as I had reached the outskirts of the brick-earth quarry district. There was no reason to head in that direction.

No reason at all.

Except...

Through the trees, in the man-made clearing beyond, lay a shrine - a shrine, a religious draw-card in the middle of destruction, keeping people content and hard-working despite the lack of a taverna.

Well, it was worth a look for the sake of research, I supposed. I'd come all this way, after all. It stood alone, and yet surrounded by offerings. A foundation of brick, atop of which was a crude stone carving of the helmet-bearing head of a goddess that shook me to the core.

Minerva had made her entrance to my unwanted, unlooked-for nature hike.

Was it a sign? Was she stepping in as Memor and Tiber had failed to help me? Was she guiding me on her path of righteousness as I sought to fulfil the curse for which she had been summoned, like some sort of freelancing deity-for-hire?

I was about to find out.

"Oi! Who are you?"

The voice was gruff. It was angry, and it meant business. I had seconds to come up with a story.

"Shrine inspector," I said as I spun around to face him. The part of my soul that dealt with emergencies did not have an overly-active imagination. The man was tall, easily a full head over myself, with muscles built from years of hard work and constant movement - lean and sinewy. Bulk-for-bulk, it would be tempting to think that I could take him, but that was as far from reality as me becoming Emperor. I had but one chance.

Bluffing.

"What?"

"I represent the Temple of Sulis Minerva." Technically, that bit was true, but I didn't elaborate in what capacity. I returned my attention to the shrine and rubbed my chin. "A nice but rustic affair, I'd say. I don't know about it though. Would you say it is fit for purpose?"

The man scowled. "The temple can keep their noses out of it," he said. "They've got no right to meddle here."

"Meddle?" I did my best to look affronted.

"This is a private site of worship for the clay diggers, not some contrived regime led by some poncy priest."

I chuckled. This man would get along with Varro-with-the-gimpy-leg. "You sound like a friend of mine. My name's Calvus." I stuck out my hand. He did not take it. "Actually, shrine inspector's only a side hustle. I live down river and got it into my head to do some exploring."

"Down river?" He raised an eyebrow. "You wouldn't happen to know Eratosthenes, would you?"

Thank you, Minerva.

"Eratosthenes? He was my neighbour."

"Was? Where is he now? Did he move or something? He was meant to do his next inspection a few days ago."

Oh, Hades! He didn't know about Eratosthenes' untimely demise. Should I tell him? What inspection?

No. No, I had a better idea.

"Oh that?" I waved my hand dismissively in his direction. "Sorry, I should have said. He asked me to do it for him, he's been so busy lately he hasn't managed to get here. You know, what with me being an inspector and all."

The man looked sceptical, so I prattled on. Which words would gain the trust of a quarryman?

"Yeah, he told me to head north up the river. But then he droned on and on about something. Sorry, I think my mind shut down there for a while, you know how he is. Something to do with brick density or the like, I think. He came up with a whole lot of numbers that I didn't understand, to be honest. In intense, minute detail." As I spoke, I thought about a conversation I had once had with Eratosthenes, in which he had told me all about the drains of some place called Arabia Petraea, and I let my face take on the same deadpan look it had adopted at the time.

It worked. Convinced that I had spoken to the real Eratosthenes, the man perked up. "Really? Great. In that case, it's this way."

13

The man, whose name was Cocceius Nonnus, was the foreman of this particular quarry and he took his job seriously. Slaves go in, mud comes out. But not just any mud. They were after the "homogeneous blue-grey clay free of alluvial sand and gravel for the maximum structural integrity of the resulting brick."

I could see why this man got along with Eratosthenes. He led me further north again, up hill and away from the river.

It was becoming urgent that I should have a private word with Minerva. She was guiding my way, and I appreciated that. But she had to get over this idea that all of her heroes were of the type that abided physical exercise. Two of the previous position-holders, Perseus and Hercules, were the sons of Jupiter, and Ulysses, her mortal champion of choice, had palaces and armies at his disposal. I was starting from a bit of a disadvantage here.

"We're coming up to it now," Nonnus said as the path, worn through years of use, sloped down into a disused quarry pit. The walls of the pit looped around and in front of us to about twice our height, opening up behind us to view the river below. At the far end, a cavity had been dug, a narrow doorway into the cliff.

"Apparently he's sending the plasterers in next week?" Nonnus looked to me and I shrugged.

"Sorry, he just said to come check it out, I don't know what's been planned."

He threw me a disappointed look. "Right. No matter. Come on inside then." The doorway was narrow and it was all Nonnus could do to get his shoulders through. "It's been a right rough time for the boys, getting this done, I tell you. Still, they've made themselves proud. Reckon they've earned a half day off, they have."

Before letting me enter behind him, he reached up to a shelf on the wall and brought down a flint and several lamps, working to get them lit before he gestured me inside and passed me one. I stashed my sack near the entrance and stepped into the passageway. What I saw took my breath away.

It was narrow, without a doubt, and straight. The walls and ceiling were lined with bricks, but not just any bricks. Anywhere the light hit, they sparkled.

"Is that... gold?"

Nonnus snorted. "No such luck. Pyrite. Looks the part. Gives the boys a right heart attack the first time they find a chunk. Think they've found the solution to all their problems. But it's not. Just some trick of the gods, little shiny rocks in the ground to give them all a laugh."

"So you leave it in the brick?"

"Not normally." He ran his hand across the wall and shook his head. "Eratosthenes has a budget to stick to. These'll do for what he needs, but I'm glad he's covering them over. Shoddy work."

Nonnus needed to rethink his outlook on business. Brickwork that sparkled gold? He'd make a fortune.

"Watch yourself," he said, gesturing onwards. "It gets a bit steep up ahead."

He wasn't kidding. Several strides in, the floor dropped vertically. The depth looked to be twice the height of a man. Without a lamp and forewarning, it would be impossible to see. Rope ladders had been fixed to the top, which Nonnus rolled out and dropped down. He double checked the pegs holding the end fast.

"He's very particular about his drop. Don't want anyone getting in, he said."

Getting in wouldn't be the problem, I thought. Getting out

with two broken ankles would be another story.

We scrambled down and continued onwards, the tunnel sloping gently downwards as we went deeper, until it opened out into a wider chamber. Nonnus moved around the room, lighting lanterns that had been left scattered around the walls. The vault looked perfectly square, about four paces wide, with an arched ceiling.

"You carved all this out for Eratosthenes?" I asked.

He nodded as he looked around with pride. "Took the boys a while, but it's not as hard as you'd think. The clay stone down here is soft, better than chipping away at that granite stuff. Wet too, but Eratosthenes had thought that through." He nodded to the arched ceiling above us. "The curved shape allows water to run down the sides rather than bearing down in the middle, and there's a whole layer of broken up rocks between the bricks and the cavity walls proper. That'll assist with drainage, according to him. He thinks about this stuff a lot. Even designed some kind of special ladder for the entrance, that would allow easy passage for the diggers with their loads of rock to cart away, but he took so long drawing up the plans that the boys just threw a rope down and got on with business. Whole chamber was done before he'd finished his concept."

That sounded like Eratosthenes alright. Bureaucratic to the point of paralysis.

It was sparsely furnished. A couple of three-legged stools in the corner. A few mortar-stiffened rags scattered about. But, standing at attention along the wall opposite the door were five familiar objects. Five little dolls, little girls and boys, the set from which the one in Jovina's shed seemed to belong.

I picked one up and turned it over in my hands. They were small but well carved, the labour of a skilled artisan. The sort of toys an uncle might buy for his orphaned niece.

"Did Eratosthenes ever tell you what all this was for?" I

asked.

"Nah. But he paid well enough, so I didn't ask questions."

"How much did he pay?"

Nonnus named the sum, and that black, tunnel vision that I had experienced earlier returned. It was more money than had perhaps passed through my hands in my lifetime. Nonnus saw the look on my face and turned defensive.

"Well, we've closed off this part of the quarry for him. Permanently. It's been two or three of my boys every day for months. And we've had to put up with his ridiculous requests of 'waiting for the time to be right', or some such nonsense."

"What does that mean?"

"It means he keeps closing the site off to us when he has some sort of other business in here. I mean, that's fine and all, but it blows out my schedule no end. When's he going to get this done? Why's he sending agents to see me now instead of coming himself?"

I swallowed, and took the risk. "He isn't sending agents. He's dead. Died weeks ago."

"What?"

"I'm trying to sort out what happened. What was going on in his life that led to his death."

Nonnus added a long list to the number of profane words that I now had stored in my vocabulary.

"Then get out and do just that," he yelled as he hustled me towards the exit. "I want my money. I don't care what's left of his estate, I want my last bill paid!"

I have never scrambled up a tunnel wall so fast in my life. Actually, I've never scrambled up a tunnel wall, but still. With Nonnus behind me, I fled.

***

I don't remember grabbing my sack of stuff as I dashed out of the passageway.

I don't remember finding the road back to Londinium.

I do remember stopping to pee along the way, but I don't remember reaching the workshop and slipping into the yard just as Tiber and Nux were packing up for the day and tucking my sack out of sight. The next memory I have was of Tiber's perplexed expression wavering into my vision.

"What are you doing here?" he asked.

"I work here."

"Do you?"

I sighed and rubbed my face.

"Sorry. You're right," I said. That raised some eyebrows.

"I'm sorry, I'm what? Not sure I heard right."

"Don't push your luck, Tiber." I glanced around. The ovens were cool and the blow pipes packed away. "What's on tomorrow?"

His eyes narrowed. "Just a shop day."

"Then you and Nux head home" – I snatched the broom from his hands – "and I'll finish up here. And I'll open up tomorrow. Give you two a well-deserved rest."

Tiber and Nux exchanged glances.

"Who are you, and what have you done with Calvus?"

"Oh, shut up." I jabbed the broom at the floor. Tiber chuckled.

"All right, then." Ever the optimist, he proceeded to recite an ambitious set of chores.

Once they'd left, I went inside and tossed the broom in the corner. We kept Nux's furnace-night-sleeping-pallet stashed upright between the shelves and the wall, so I slid it out, set it up, and took a moment to rest my weary bones before starting on the true work of the evening.

Man alive. Six weeks ago, coercion had led to my presence at the funeral of a neighbour; a funeral met with a socially acceptable level of grief and remorse at a sorry situation, mixed in with an incongruous level of shame and relief when it dawned on me that I would never have to sit through another micro-focused discussion on the architectural merits of... hang on, I know this... Dojiser Dojiseroo? Jeeer Gesaru? Old Geezer Shrew?

Okay, so I don't know it. But what did it matter any more? The man was dead.

Since that time I had angered a potential murderer, become besties with the effective head of a religion, given hypothetical birth to a god, discovered that my deceased neighbour had a much more eccentric and potentially nefarious lifestyle than I gave him credit for, and been sent scurrying by a pissed-off quarryman who rued unpaid bills more than he regretted untimely deaths.

Oh, and I had lost a wooden spoon but in the grand scheme of things, that probably wasn't a big issue. Come on, let's keep some perspective here.

Perspective, and momentum. And right now, that momentum was needed to keep me alive for the night. I would not be returning home. Nux's pallet would suffice for now. I doubted Tiber would agree, but Tiber wasn't here.

Nux was fortunate. Any other slave would have been allotted a woven mat on the floor, but that was simply unacceptable for Tiber's wife, Enica. Her gentle but firm nudging of her husband had seen Tiber's brief foray into alternative crafts, in this case woodworking, to give rise to a low but serviceable bed frame for Nux. This bore a woollen yarn webbing, lovingly spun and woven by Enica herself, which in turn supported a comfortably thick, straw-stuffed mattress. One day, Nux may be surprised to discover that his luxurious bed was missing, swapped out for a rather older, wood-wormy version with multiple broken strings, if I could figure out how to make the exchange from my house without having to personally manhandle two bed frames across town on roughly cobbled streets and muddy switchbacks.

I retrieved my sack and spread out my blanket. As a home-away-from-home, it lacked a certain, well, homeliness. As a bolt-hole from a child-stealing, murderous maniac, it would suffice, with a few more finishing touches.

Before the sun could dip below the horizon, I lit every lamp we possessed and built a box-fort around the bed. Tiber's collection of blow pipes formed a crafty, if moderately unstable, palisade wall. One might say that that was going overboard, but if one's life was in danger, one would agree with me that it was adequate at best. I walked the perimeter of the shop and warehouse. Everything was locked and bolted.

I was safe—

There was a knock at the front door.

Ah, Hades. What was I meant to do now? An assassin would be unlikely to announce their presence. They'd come in the back way, quietly.

Unless that's what they wanted me to think.

But what if they wanted me to think that's what they wanted me to think? What if it was a decoy knock, to send me fleeing out the back to meet my fate?

I danced on the spot trying to reconcile that one in my head.

The tap came again, quiet but urgent.

It was time for Vitrumesh to prove his worth and protect his charge, his own creator, from the terror that lay beyond. To provide me with a sign of what was to come, be they friend or foe. I sidled though the interconnecting door and into the shop. I stared at the front door, eyes bulging and eyebrows furrowed in my effort to render the wood invisible, and waited for that sign to come.

It turns out that my made-up-god-given-abilities did not

include being able to see through solid matter. This time, even Minerva had not seen fit to step in and help, even though she owed me one, big time.

Nothing else for it, I guess. I picked up a vase to smash over the head of my would-be assailant - with my silent apologies to Tiber, but a broken vase was better than a broken partner - and unlatched the door.

"Titus?"

"Marcella?"

I threw the door wide and there she stood, cloaked against the cold in the dark, and ostensibly alone. "Why are you here? How—"

"Let me in, will you?" She shivered.

I hastened to put the vase down so that I could guide her through the door with my hand across the back of her shoulders. Even through the thick cloak, I could sense her petite form. Despite everything, that slight touch of her body thrilled me, all thoughts of my previous feelings of impending doom fled from my mind.

"Your description of the glass, I had to come see, and... oh, my goodness." She stood and stared around the room.

The shop was lit by easily a dozen lamps. The flames flickered in the draft as I pushed the door closed and replaced the latch.

Hues of red, yellow, blue and green jittered around the walls so I let her admire the effect for a moment before asking, "Are you here alone?"

She nodded. "Problem?"

"Well, your uncle..."

"...doesn't need to know." She glanced at me with a grin, but her eyes moved on immediately to a pitcher on the shelf behind me. She recognised quality. Translucent red, its circular foot held aloft a round body decorated with a local knotwork design. The whole thing tapered up to a narrow neck with an elaborate looped handle for pouring.

"Is that one of yours?"

"Yes," I lied, subtly positioning myself between her and the bargain table. "Marcella, you shouldn't be out at night like this, it's not safe—"

"Urgh," she groaned. "You sound like Uncle Lucius."

"Do you sneak out often?"

"Of course not." She moved around the room, brushing her fingers across bowls and bottles alike. "But it's just so exciting, don't you think?"

"Exciting?"

"Londinium." She glanced at me, her eyes wide. "There's so much to see. You're so lucky to live here. Can you imagine what Hesiod would have written had he been here? Oh, or Ovid?"

"Marcella, Londinium has docks and markets, an amphitheatre and a palace—"

"Oh, a palace!"

"—but nothing that outshines Aquae Sulis and nothing that can't wait until morning, in the light—"

"Uncle Lucius says that in Rome, they have learnt the secret of truly clear glass that's being used in the windows of the most luxurious villas of the Campagna. Can you do that?"

I had heard tales of this clear window glass, and thought it nothing more than the result of an escalating "my villa's better than your villa" competition. I could almost picture the scene, two mega-wealthy senators in the hot bath, elbows hooked over the side, blinded by the chandelier light bouncing off gold veined marble. Men, whose 'eccentricities' were identical to the 'depravities' of the ultra-poor, but with that much money behind them, who was going to complain?

"Mine," says one, "on the outskirts of Baiae, overlooks the villa once owned by Julius Caesar. Hadrian himself now takes his rest in there, below. Imagine that, looking down upon the villa of emperors. The view gives a sense of perspective that calms the soul. Neptune's domain stretches as far as it does wide, dolphins dance in the rose-red light of Sol's evening retreat. With such vastness of divinity on display, how can the problems of man seem anything but small?"

"Now, that," responds the other, "sounds like the view just from my toilet alone. Which I look at, while sitting there in moments of urgency, gazing through clear glass windows."

But, I wouldn't discredit Memor to his niece in that way.

"Sadly," I responded, "that is a secret that has yet to grace the shores of Britannia."

She pouted but let it lie. "Show me where you make all this."

I led her through to the workshop and she poked around various piles of tools and materials with interest, but if she saw my box-fort bed, she didn't comment on it.

"Marcella, why are you here?"

"I told you, to see the glass."

"No," I shook my head. "There's plenty of time during the day for that, when the shop is open."

She turned but did not say a word. She didn't have too. She stepped closer. Her hand raised itself to my cheek. The kiss was long, deep, and ongoing, as the blow-pipe palisade collapsed around us.

14

What, you want a description of what happened next?
Mind your own business.

15

I will say one thing about what happened. A one-person cot surrounded by blowpipes and boxes makes it awfully awkward.

I lay on the ground; Marcella regarded me from upon the cot. I lay panting, she lay snuggled up under my blanket. Our clothes lay... somewhere. That was a problem for later. She giggled.

"Well, that was unexpected," she said. She blushed as she rolled back onto her back to stare at the ceiling. "I just wish..."

I sat bolt upright.

"Was the war-cry too much?"

"No, of course not," she laughed. To show me how little that mattered to her, she did a wondrous thing. She joined me on the floor. It is true love indeed if your lover ventures out from the warm safety of a thick woollen blanket to be with you. And it is love eternal if you allow her to push you back down, lying with no thought given to the chill against your back. She straddled my stomach, her knees bearing the solidity of the coarse concrete without complaint.

I reached up and ran my fingers across the small birthmark on her pelvis and up her side, to brush her hair back from her now goosepimply shoulders.

"It's just... well" – she said as I guided her face downwards to meet mine – "I'm to be married next month."

I blinked and let my hand drop.

"You know, your second-round seduction technique needs some work," I said.

"Oh, there'll be a second round."

"Marcella..."

"He's not like you," she continued with a pout of disgust. "A stuffy young officer all set to become a stuffy old senator. Who wants to be stuck with that?" She pushed a wayward curl back from her forehead, tucking it behind her ear as the lamplight bounced off her broad, hinged, gold strip bracelet, set with turquoise cabochon reminiscent of the colours in Memor's atrium.

"Marcella, you're the eligible ward of a man who has privately commissioned artwork, a house that's recognised as a local landmark, and with a profound lack of interest in the opinion of others."

"So?"

"So, it's going to be my name scratched with cuckolded ferocity into lead, sinking into the depths of the Sacred Spring."

She leant down and kissed me, and damn me but I couldn't resist. The moment stretched on, until she pulled back and murmured - "I could talk to Uncle Lucius."

"Talk to your uncle?"

"You could be the husband of his eligible ward."

"Oh, Marcella. I love your optimism."

The face she pulled was not pretty. The chill flooded my body as she retreated back to the cot with its blanket. She pulled it around her, hiding her body from view.

Aww.

"And does what I want matter to no-one here?" she asked.

"I'm sorry?"

"Oh, what do you think?"

No-one should ever ask me that question. The instant that question falls from someone's lips, my mind is instantly wiped clean of all thought.

"Ah..."

She rolled her eyes. "That figures."

"I'm sorry, but I don't know what you mean."

"Of course you don't. Because you'd just follow along with Uncle Lucius' plans. Marry well, and baby-sit the stone head of an Empress as the newest initiate in the Imperial Cult's priesthood. And spin, and weave, and bear an ocean of children to do the same. What if it's not what I want? What if I want you?"

"Oh, Marcella," my heart sank as I sat up. "And I would have you. I don't want this to just be a memory. I want to be the one to kill spiders for you and to fight with you about keeping my dining couch. But it's just not possible."

"Yeah, right."

"No, look around you. Your uncle can marry you to whoever he likes. I would make you a twisted glass bracelet, but it would be just a poor trinket compared to what you could have. I can't compete."

She pouted and looked around. After a moment, she broke the silence that had formed between us.

"Why do you think my father married my mother?"

"He seemed to really love her."

"Not at first. He married her because of her family. Uncle Lucius is not the first to follow the path of haruspicy."

"He married her to be close to Memor?"

"My father married into religious power. He was nuts for it, the full thing. The gods, the wonder, the magic, the awe. We have a statue of an Oceanid in our atrium, for crying out loud."

She rose and drifted around the room, running her fingers over this and that as she thought.

"What did your mother think about that?" I asked. "Having her face on the epitome of maternity?"

She chuckled, but it was not a happy sound.

"I suppose that would have been quite the pressure. To be the next mother of fifty. But..." she sighed. "But never mind that. Look, maybe..." she sighed. "Maybe once all this is done, once you have shown Uncle Lucius your value, your talent at completing the task he gave you, the power that you would give us by bringing our family close to the cult of Vitru... that god, then maybe he'd consider it. And maybe, in time, he would come to love you too. How close are you to finding her?"

I winced. "It's not as simple as just a kidnapping any more."

I moved up to sit on the edge of the cot - there's only so much chill even my young joints could take alone on the floor, and described to her what I had found to date. I spoke of it as gently as I could, but her face grew ashen as I described the underground cell and the death of the man who'd created it.

"Do you have any idea why Jovina would want to take Vilbia?" I asked.

She shrugged as she sank back down beside me. "She always got along well with Vilbia, when we saw her at the bathhouse. Maybe Vilbia asked her for help to run away."

"But is that enough reason for Jovina to go with her? It's one thing to help her climb out the window, and then there's giving up your life to run away with her."

"Then, maybe Jovina had other reasons. That room, the one in the cliff, you said there was no way out except the rope ladder?"

"Yes."

"So, it could be used to hold someone, to stop them running away?"

"Yes, but why—"

"Like a slave? Or someone about to become a slave?"

It could be that Jovina had seen an opportunity out of poverty. A young girl, eager to flee from her family and trusting of the priestess who offered help, but of high value to the traders who frequented Londinium's ports. If that was the case, Vilbia may never be found. Marcella read my thoughts.

"She's still nearby," she said.

"Marcella, I think we need to consider that she has long departed Britannia."

"No," she said. "Don't give me that look. There's a good reason to think she is still nearby. That room you found."

"What do you mean?"

"If you had tricked a child to sell for easy cash, would you custom-build a holding cell for them? Underground? Dug out of the rock?"

"Fair point. But why—"

"Here's what I think happened." Marcella was on a roll now, and would not be stopped. "I think Jovina saw the wealth of those who come to the Temple. She was jealous, and wanted to take some of that wealth for herself. I think Jovina knew Vilbia wanted to run away, and saw the opportunity to trick her, sell her into slavery, and keep the money. They came to Londinium, but something happened. Jovina married this other man. Erot..."

"Eratosthenes."

She pulled a face. "Yeah, him. Whatever happened, they kept Vilbia, making her a cell from which she couldn't escape. They kept her as their own slave. But now they know you're on to them. They see her as stolen goods. They're moving her around."

In her mind, Eratosthenes wasn't a victim. Eratosthenes was a part of it. Whatever 'it' was. He had known about Vilbia. He had helped to hide her, constructing a cell in the rock that was impossible to get out of without a ladder. He had kept the quarry workers away whenever they had need to stash her in there. But why did they need to move her around, and where was she now?

And how in Hades could they have afforded to have Nonnus and his quarry crew build them the cell in the first place?

"Marcella, none of this is making any sense. I can see why you want it to believe it, but... I just don't know."

"Can you even be sure that this Erotenese is dead?"

I didn't answer but my mind whirled.

Okay, let's go over this again. What was that list that I had devised as compelling evidence of a murder?

A body.

We only had the word of Jovina and Petronax that the missing body of Eratosthenes was actually in the form of a cadaver, and not the living, breathing body of a husband and insurance premium-payer. But why was I taking their word for this - a woman suspected of kidnap and a priest who cheated his congregation?

A plausible motive.

Jovina could have murdered Eratosthenes in an argument over Vilbia, but realistically she could also have decided just to do the deed to make way for her lover, Augustalis. But a motive does not a crime make.

An eyewitness to the event.

No-one had yet come forward.

A bloody knife, or a frying pan with Eratosthenes' fine Egyptian nose protruding forth.

Still nope.

I was no further forward on the murder-case-front, but I did have additional evidence. I had discovered a secret location that Eratosthenes had been constructing, or at least providing painstaking instructions as to its construction. And I had someone very keen to threaten me, smashing my belongings in an attempt to see me off investigating further.

I think I had just learnt the first lesson that any decent informer learns on their first day of spy school. Just because you are told that a person is dead, does not mean that they are in fact, dead.

***

I awoke to a stream of water splashing on my face.

"Get him again," came Tiber's voice. Spluttering, I opened my eyes to two depressingly bright phenomena - the sunlight, and Nux's facial expression, right before copping the remaining liquid in his cup right on the bridge of my nose.

"Knock it off!" I fell off the cot and onto the concrete. Tangled up in the blanket as I was, escape was futile. Nux had reason to thank that blanket - the brutal defence of my person proved ineffective as my flailing arm failed to make contact with his shins.

"You had one job to do, Calvus," said Tiber.

"Cleaning up is a series of jobs, all linked together under one heading," I pointed out as I struggled to my feet.

"And which of that series of jobs involved making an obstacle course and leaving your loincloth draped across the soda pots?"

"I need to pee." I hastened towards the back door, pulling my tunic over my head and gathering up my remaining clothes as I did so. I was relieved that Marcella seemed to have already made good her escape, but when Tiber followed me out to ensure that I did not do the same, it became apparent that I would genuinely have to suffice with the bladder version of relief for myself.

Mid-stream behind the cooling oven was perhaps not the right time or place for the discussion that followed, but it was the time and place that Tiber chose.

"This isn't working out, Calvus."

I glanced at him. He was standing uncomfortably close.

"No, maybe you should take a step back or eight."

He grunted and edged around, giving me a semblance of privacy, but we were still hunkered together like a pair of budget-grade conspirators. He had the decency to look uncomfortable, at least.

"When we..." he paused and cleared his throat. "When we went into partnership—"

"Ha!" I laughed. "So I am a partner, not an apprentice? In your face, Nux."

"Don't do that, Calvus. When we went into partnership here, that meant you did half the work."

"Oh come on, Tiber, I've been busy."

"On what?" He looked back at me, but it didn't matter any more, I had moved on to pulling on my sandals. "This new religion of yours?"

"I'm on the verge of something. It's going to be—"

"Big? Grandiose? Profitable?"

"Exactly."

"Not informative, meaningful, inspiring?"

"That's not fair." I pushed past him to go back inside, but he grabbed my arm. Nux took two steps out the door on a mission to empty a cleaning bucket, saw us, spun on his heel and went straight back inside.

"What do you want to get out of this, Calvus?"

"What do you mean?"

"What are the material benefits that Calvus receives from this sham?"

I baulked. "Sham?"

"Yes, that's exactly what it is," he said. "Are you already rich?"

"What? No, of course not."

"Then you can't help to pull others up. Were you downtrodden? Can you show people the path out?"

"Tiber—"

"No? You just want something for yourself and you don't care about the hurt that causes."

"Hurt?" That was rich. "I want to help people—"

"By lying to them and taking advantage of their beliefs?"

"Bah!" I spun away, both my hands on the top of my head as I looked to the sky above. My mind raced but my eyes followed the flight of a flock of geese, flying in a V-shaped formation in the dawn light, towards the sun as it warmed up to being a brilliant day. Somewhere, an augur was reading that as an omen, passing on a message of hope to those who had sought his help. Somewhere, across the river, Petronax was offering week-old meat on a spit roast to his congregated crowds, giving them the courage to continue on with their lives safe in the knowledge that the gods were appeased. The truth behind their satiated bellies was not helpful, that the meat that they ate was not the sacrifice that they had just witnessed and a gift from the joyful gods themselves, but instead it was meat that had been deliberately aged by mortals in a cellar to bring about the tenderness of its texture.

The feeling of hope, connection and stability that the ritual imparted was the important thing. The deception was just a means to an end.

I just didn't know how to get Tiber to see it that way.

"I'm trying to help people now, that's why I've been away..."

I didn't need to look to hear the grimace in his voice. "You've been meddling in some poor family's sorry situation, giving them false hope that you can find their loved one. What are they giving you in return? What happens when you can't? Do you just say sorry and walk away? Beyond what they have told you, do you even have a clue what is going on—"

"Eratosthenes is alive."

"What?"

I turned to face him. His face bore an incredulous expression.

"Eratosthenes is alive," I repeated, convinced of the matter. "They're all in it together. I've found evidence that he and Jovina were keeping the girl captive. They're going to sell her—"

"Listen to yourself, Calvus." That was too much for him. He closed his eyes and hung his head, catching his breath. When he spoke, his voice was low and carefully spoken, cracking just here and there. "You're obsessing over this fantasy, spouting nonsense about murders and gods and curses. Now your murder victim has come back to life. I'm done, Calvus. I'm going to start looking for a new workshop.

"What happened to making true Britannic glass together, Tiber?"

"You were never going to go for that, anyway. There's some workshops up beyond the fort that may have me join them."

"You know what? Fine."

I left, vaulting over the back wall, determined to see this mystery through.

<h1 style="text-align:center">16</h1>

I had to find Eratosthenes. Only by dragging him kicking and screaming into the workshop would I convince Tiber that something big was happening and to get him off this silly tangent of moving elsewhere. Oh, and it would enable me to find Vilbia, win over Memor, marry Marcella, and be rewarded with Memor's land for my temple.

So, no biggie, but Eratosthenes was now the key to everything.

There was one person who might help me, and that person would either try to kill me, or sell me funeral insurance. I'm not sure which I preferred.

Petronax.

I went prepared for both. Tucked away under my belt was a dagger and a list of all the other people who wanted me dead, starting with my father and ending with Tiber. Nothing would shut down the promise of a long life of premium payments like a list of imminent murder suspects.

As I crossed the river, I rehearsed the conversation.

"So, Petronax, I know you colluded with Jovina..."

No.

"Hey, Petronax. Just need to catch up with Eratosthenes. What? Dead, you say? No, no, it's all right. I know everything..."

No.

"Hi Petronax. So, I know a magician never reveals his tricks, but how did you make Eratosthenes disappear?"

I was a dead man.

The temple complex of Mars Camulus and the Imperial Cult swung into view. Today, the scene was peaceful. There was no pious gathering by the river's edge, and, more importantly, no guards at the gate. There was no need for stealth or subterfuge as I strolled into the yard.

One day, I would have all this.

Well, not this, but something similar. But mine would be different. Better. More gardens, I think. Vitrumesh loves gardens. All that...

Ah...

Well, I was sure I could think of a reason for him to love gardens. I had time to work on that. I ambled through the paved yard, dipping my head to other visitors who happened to cast glances in my direction, and intending to inspect the outdoor altar. As the central point of public worship beyond the off-limits temple sanctum, it was an important feature to get right, and I intended to inspect as many as possible before devising my own design. I had witnessed Memor and Petronax performing their sacrifices the last time I was here, but today it served the function of a simple votive altar from which the public could present their own humble offerings to the gods. A woman stood there now, her back to me, the back of her shawl pulled up over her head in religious respect, awaiting some symbol or sign to start her ritual.

My date with death or destiny at Petronax's hands could wait. I sidled over to the columns of the temple itself, ostensibly to give the woman some privacy as she performed her rites, whilst enjoying the comfort of the shade provided by the verandah awning above me.

As I settled into position, Memor himself exited the temple sanctum, bearing aloft a portable statue of a god. Why Memor was here, assisting with private rites and not Petronax was a bit of a mystery. Perhaps Petronax was unavailable? Maybe he was out shopping for next week's roasted offerings? Maybe he was off doing something sinister with Jovina and Eratosthenes.

Whatever the reason, Memor was covering his duties. It

would probably be a good opportunity to fill him in on where things were at, excluding where things were at with his niece, of course, so I resolved to wait until he was free.

He carried the little statue to the altar, placing it down on the stone with reverence. Its features were hard to see, but it looked like a little deified emperor rather than a little Olympic god.

Claudius, perhaps? He was big in these parts and had a temple all to himself in the nearby town of Camulodunum. A temple of his own, with no need to share it with his fractious family, those who had snubbed him for his afflictions: Claudius, the drooling, stammering, weak-kneed boy, ignored because they had thought him pitiful. But he outlived them all, side-stepping all the stabbings, poisonings and suffocations that occurred with alarming frequency around him to become Emperor in his own right.

Nor did he share that temple with his great-nephew, son-in-law, and step-son combined, Nero, whose mother, Claudius' wife and niece, Agrippina, murdered Claudius to see her son take up the reign, so-to-speak.

Julio-Claudian family reunions must be confusing at best, and that's without everyone trying to kill each other.

But I digress.

Credited with the conquest of Britannia, it would seem reasonable that it was the deified Claudius who was deemed worthy of individual worship today.

It was a ritual with which I was familiar. As Memor stepped back, the worshipper lit incense before the statue, muttering words carried to the god in the smoke. I had watched my father perform this rite often, in our home, upon the family shrine in the courtyard. It was a ritual that I had lapsed in performing myself since departing Rome. There just never seemed to be the time, so I hoped and trusted that Father continued on in my stead, placating the gods enough for both of us. That seemed like something he would do.

The ritual was brief and Memor whisked the statue back into the temple. As he moved away, the woman lowered her shawl back to her shoulders and turned.

It was Marcella.

I pressed myself against the column.

After last night, catching up with Memor alone was fine. Catching up with Memor with Marcella together was a moment of awkwardness that I did not have the mental capacity to deal with right now. I did not think that she would have returned to the temple; after last night, I had assumed she would have delayed in reuniting with her uncle for as long as possible.

Did he know about Marcella's break away into the night?

Could he possibly know where she had gone?

Which bone in my body would he break first if he gleaned the true nature of our relationship?

I could have stood there and concocted a plethora of excuses for the sudden onset of blushes and giggles (and that was just from me), each more implausible than the last, but there was no time. Memor had re-emerged and gestured for Marcella to follow him.

They were striding in my direction.

I slipped around the column to cross to the outer wall of the temple and hurried around to the back of the building, but to no avail.

"Around here," came Memor's voice. It sounded strained.

Logic would have me continue around the temple and out the other side, but logic plays no part in the way my mind works. My eyes fell to the one place that seemed ideal. A collection of potted plants, concealing the trap door to the temple's meat cellar. It wasn't locked. What was the point? Why would anyone have any nefarious need to go down there?

I threw myself through the hole and pulled the door after me just as the pair rounded the corner. I left it ajar - they were unlikely to look, surely? And all the better for eavesdropping.

"What have you done?" Memor's voice came in a low hiss. I couldn't see Marcella from this angle. I could, however, see Memor's face and it was the epitome of annoyance.

"What do you mean?"

"Don't play games with me, girl."

"I've been keeping myself entertained."

I almost groaned aloud at that, and Memor's eyes narrowed.

"With that pathetic priest?"

"He took me shopping."

"Shop... Marcella, where were you last night?"

"Where do you think I was? I've been doing more to get this dealt with than you have. I know—"

"You have no idea! Prying where—"

"I know there's a cell carved into the cliff."

"A what?"

"Oh," her voice took on a light and airy tone. "Didn't you know?"

Memor ran a hand over his face and spoke his next words slowly, "Where were you last night?"

"Oh..." something had dawned on Marcella. "You've got your ape involved."

"Marcella..."

"Where is he?"

"Keep it down, girl."

"Keep it down? This is my future!"

She stepped towards him. I could see her - her rigid back, almost blocking Memor's now pomegranate-red face from sight. I could swear she was about to hit him, to strike that yellowed, fleshy jowl, but for Memor's sudden move to grab her wrist, forcing her back and down until she all-but knelt before him.

"Ah!"

"Your future?" he spat. "You would throw your future away with your meddling."

Marcella crumpled before him.

"I'm sorry," she said, her voice almost a whisper.

"What was that?" Memor demanded.

"I'm... sorry."

Memor sighed. He glanced around and, with some difficulty, squatted before Marcella, bringing their faces together to the same height. He took Marcella's head in both hands and stared at her.

"Minerva is trying to help you, child, but..." he huffed in exasperation. "You just don't make it easy for her sometimes." He touched their foreheads together. "Have trust in me, Marcella."

He stood, but Marcella did not move.

"But, why is he helping? Why? He betrayed us."

"Betrayed us? Ha! Your simpleton is the one who has betrayed us."

"No—"

"He's been hiding her!"

"What?"

"My 'ape' knows where she is. And your simpleton has been keeping her from us. Leading you astray. So ask yourself, which one should we trust now?"

"But he wouldn't—"

Memor rounded on her. Marcella's eyes flew open as she raised an arm to protect herself, but he restrained his fury.

"Do you think Minerva wants this?" he demanded. "Do you think she likes to be made a fool of?"

"No."

"No! Then why do you question me? The damage that idiot has done, the damage he's done to your future, the one you so desperately want. You know what happens next. He's on his way to that fool's workshop now." He kicked a pot plant, sending dirt tumbling through the gap in the trapdoor and over my face. I fought against every instinct I had to slam the door shut, lest it reveal my hiding spot, but I remained hidden.

"A cell in a cliff?" Memor almost muttered to himself. "For all that is holy....and you believed that?"

"What about the other one?" asked Marcella.

"If he gets in the way, we'll take care of him. Come on."

***

As their voices faded, I hoisted myself out of the cellar. Broken shards of pot clattered to the floor beneath me, loud enough that surely they would come running.

I had defiled Memor's niece, and he knew. Somehow, he knew.

A woman losing her virginity before her first marriage - that could get her shunned by her groom, or worse.

Memor was on the warpath, and Tiber was in the way. I had to get to the workshop before them.

I turned and sprinted out of the gates.

***

You know what I think about people like the Athenian runner Pheidippides? The ones who can keep up a steady jog for longer than a hundred yards?

I hate them.

The thought that every double-time step I took towards the workshop put me a fraction of a moment ahead of Memor spurred me on for the full length of the two Roman miles back to the workshop, but I would not say that I arrived there in fighting-fit condition.

151

Not even in remotely fit condition.

But it didn't matter.

I was too late.

As I heaved myself through the last few steps towards the shop entrance, I still had hope. People were on errands and were wandering the streets, zigzagging their way from mill to forge to laundry. Eucarpus, the stocky farrier across the way, stood hunched over the back leg of a horse whose hoof he was manicuring with the rough edge of a file. He raised his eyes to mine briefly before hunkering back down to his work. A few others disappeared back into their shops.

The door to our shop stood ajar. Nothing unusual, it was opening hours. Nux would be inside, rehearsing his sales spiel to himself, or wrapping up a vase in a green scrap of linen, an off-cut sourced from the dressmaker a block down the road, ready to relinquish the item to the awaiting hands of a discerning agent of a wealthy customer.

I pushed the door wide to the sound of shattered glass on the floor. The veritable rainbow was no more; in its place lay an ocean of dagger-sharp shards ready to slice open any sandal-sole or knee-skin that fell their way.

"Tiber?" I waded through the room, taking care to push glass away with the side of my boot before placing my weight, to reach workshop door. My voice faltered.

"Tiber?"

The workshop fared little better. Tools and smashed pots of soda lay strewn across the floor.

There was one tool, in fact, that as it swung into my field of view, led me to think:

'Oh, there it is.'

No longer lost, my giant beer brewing spoon connected with my temple and I crumpled to the floor.

17

I was stunned, but not knocked out.

Have you ever rubbed your eyes too hard, and when you release them you get blurred, moving vision? Your displaced eyes take a moment to settle back into that patch of skull and sinew that's conformed to their shape through the years, that well-worn groove they call home.

Now, take that feeling and multiply it ten-fold.

That's what I was experiencing now, but not for the trivial moment that you experience when rubbing your eyes. It lasted easily until the count of twenty. Me, on my hands and knees, blinking as three conflicting images in my vision failed to line up.

I puked.

When the images did at last merge into one vomit-drenched spoon lying on the floor in front of me, it was joined in my field of view by something else - a walking stick, or...

"Calvus the glass-blowing, religious, beer brewing informer?"

I peered up, blood trickling from a gash in my forehead.

"Varro? What... how—?"

Varro-with-the-gimpy-leg stood above me, leaning on his crutch and giving me the sardonic eyebrow.

"Did... did you hit me?" I asked.

"'Course not. You all right?"

"I'm dying," I said, certain of my self-proclaimed fate. My head throbbed and I would never trust my legs to hold my weight again. I held my spoon against my chest like a child's toy as I curled into the foetal position and waited for the inevitable.

"You're fine," he said.

"I am dying."

"What's your name?"

"Laelius Calvus."

"And where are you?"

"In the warehouse, cuddling my stolen spoon, surrounded by my partner's broken dreams and waiting for a Sacred-Spring-defiling maniac to finish me off for bedding Memor's niece."

"Ha! You fucked Marcella? Maybe you are going to die then, but not by my hand. You're fine, get up."

"Why did you hit me?"

"I didn't. That was Augustalis."

"Augustalis?" Now I knew all this was some sort of transitioning dream as I passed into the underworld. "Where's Tiber?"

"Who's Tiber?"

"My partner. Big, robust guy. Made all of this." I swooshed my arm around as if that explained everything.

"Ain't no-one else here. Hasn't been, not since we got here."

"We?"

"Augustalis and I. Not that Augustalis knew that I was here too."

My head throbbed with the exertion of thought, so my mind sent Varro's words straight into my figurative too-hard basket without even acknowledging their existence.

"I've got to find Tiber," I said.

I struggled to get up. Varro struggled to help me. Together, we made the simple act of standing look like one of the twelve labours of Hercules.

"So, where is this Tiber?" Varro asked once he'd caught his breath.

"I... I don't..." I looked around. There was no sign of them here, and if Varro hadn't been lying, then Tiber and Nux had already left before...

"Where are you going?" Varro asked as I lurched from pot

stand to pincer shelf.

"To Tiber's house. If he's not there, he's got a legion of ankle-biters who can form a search party. And, you're coming with me." I pointed my spoon at him to emphasize the point.

"Why?"

"Because I have no idea in Hades what is going on around here but you do. You can tell me on the way."

***

We made a right pair as we lurched along, drawing out the ten-minute stroll to Tiber's into a twenty-minute test of endurance.

"How do you know Augustalis?" I asked as we hobbled down the cobbled street, sidestepping handcarts and horse dung with awkward indecision. "And, why are you here following him?"

"Well, I wasn't. Not to start with. He's one of them lot, isn't he? From the Temple. But, when I saw him with Memor, I knew Augustalis would be the one to get his hands dirty. So, I stopped following Memor and started following him instead."

"Varro?"

"Yes?"

"You're not helping my headache. Can you start from the beginning?"

"Fine. Now, remember asking me about Jovina at Minerva's Temple, or did that knock on the head make you forget?"

"I remember. You described someone who was definitely not the Jovina I know, so I thanked you and left."

He waved a hand in dismissal and made that funny little 'pfft' sound that people make when you've said something so far below their regard that it doesn't even warrant a coherent syllable.

155

"You got me thinking," he said, "and I wanted to help, so I've been following Memor."

"Why would you do that?"

"Why wouldn't I? We all know the story about Vilbia. We all know that she and Jovina were friends. So, there's only one person who'd have hired you to track her down."

I grimaced with the strain of thought. "Okay, but why follow Memor? I'm working for him, not against him."

"Didn't say I wanted to help you, did I? Besides, it's pretty obvious you only think you work for him."

"I'm pretty certain I do. I'm getting paid."

"In money?"

"In land, actually."

He snorted. "And you've seen this land and inspected it?"

"Just get on with your story."

"Right, well, I followed Memor home that day. Calm as you like, that chubby haruspex pulled his steward aside and told him to get packing, then he, you and Marcella ambled on, off to Londinium the next morning. But, it wasn't a planned trip. Memor might have been calm, but his slaves certainly weren't. An unannounced trip to Londinium? It threw his little entourage into such a tizzy to get ready as you wouldn't believe."

"But," I said, "he told me in the changing room that he had been called to Londinium."

"Then either he was informed about it while nude or he decided on the spot to keep you close to him, even if that meant abandoning his plans for a relaxing week of cursing the populace for minor indiscretions and travelling with you to Londinium. I hitched a ride with a merchant friend of mine and we followed along. Memor's been staying at that mansio near to that Temple of Camulus and the Imperial Nutcases, and yesterday morning he met up with Augustalis.

"It wasn't a happy meeting. When they parted, as I said, I

followed Augustalis. He took me on a straight path through the city. Smashed up some poor bugger's house in a valley to the north. Oh..." he took in the way my jaw jutted. "Was that yours, too?"

"Just get on with it," I replied.

He shrugged as we made way for a hand cart coming the other direction down the road, laden with fabrics presumably bound for a nearby laundry.

"Not much else to tell. Augustalis did the rounds of a few tavernas last night, nursed his head this morning, tore through your workshop, you turned up shortly after, and here we are."

"You've been lurching around after Memor and Augustalis for days now? Didn't they notice you?"

He snorted again. "What do you do when you see someone with an obvious physical difference walking down the road?"

"Huh?"

"Kids stare at me. Some of them ask me for all the gory details about how my leg got busted up, and I'm happy to tell 'em, too. It keeps 'em up at night crying and I get the satisfaction in knowing I've made some poor mother's life a misery.

"But adults avert their eyes, either out of disgust or because they think they're being polite. Either way, most get it down to such a fine art that not looking at people who are different has become an unconscious reflex. I'm well outside of Augustalis' field of view."

"That's awful... well, handy at the moment, but awful all the same."

He shrugged. He was right, though. As we passed houses and veggie gardens, no-one looked our way, except for one kid with his finger up his nose and whose eyes never left us for a second. One of us was waddling along with his stick as if dancing to music the rest of us couldn't hear, and the other was holding a saturated bloody rag to the side of his face. That should be cause for concern, but no-one looked; no-one wanted to make eye contact and be drawn into an uncomfortable situation.

"Wait," I continued. "Augustalis has been trying to get me for days now? But I only slept with Marcella last night."

"Seems they've found some entirely different reason to hate you."

A few paces on, and I had reached a horrible conclusion.

"I'm not getting my land, am I?"

"I have my doubts."

We walked the remaining distance in silence until we came upon the cluster of buildings nestled in near the fort, and the doorway that was set back in an alcove leading to the space that Tiber called home.

I let us in without knocking. This was in no way a reflection of Nux's ability as a doorman even though I suspected that he would take great pleasure in letting me wait on the doorstep, risking my life. It was due to the layout of Tiber's house. The portion that faced onto the street was in fact Tiber's original workshop – a space he now rented to his carpenter neighbour as storage. The family lived in the rooms at the back, with no chance of hearing visitors arrive. Those who knew them, knew to go through to the back. Those who didn't...well, Tiber probably didn't want to talk to them anyway.

Just enough light came through the shuttered windows that I could lead the way through the stacked planks and oak beams, my spoon held out in front of me like a sword.

"Expecting bad guys, are we?" asked Varro from behind me. "What are you going to do with that? Poison 'em with soup?"

I ignored him and we made it to the far end with relatively few stubbed toes. I leant on the connecting door, easing it open. There was no use bursting in and startling anyone inside, be they friend or foe, if it meant that I would earn a doubly-dented head courtesy of a fry-pan.

"Tiber?" I called out.

The voice that responded was not Tiber's, nor was it even male. But it sounded disappointed, none-the-less.

"Calvus."

"Jovina?"

I pushed my way into the space that served as both kitchen and dining room, and there she was, staring at me from the far end of the heavy wooden dining table. I levelled my spoon at her. She looked back at me, puzzled.

"Calvus?"

"Jovina."

"Lovely lady!" Varro-with-the-gimpy-leg beamed as he entered behind me.

"Varro?"

"Jovina."

"You bloody idiot."

That last one was Tiber as he, too, stormed into the room, emerging from the corridor that led off to the bedrooms. He wrestled the spoon from my hand and threw it to the floor. It clattered under a cupboard but we weren't done shouting names at each other yet.

"Tiber!"

Tiber's wife Enica entered behind him and blanched at the state of my head. "Calvus...oh my goodness!"

She was accompanied by...

"Pac—"

"Vilbia!"

"What?"

I spun away from Enica's motherly hands, which were prizing the sodden rag away from my face and stared at Varro.

"What did you say?"

He held his hand palm up and gestured to Pacatus.

"That's Vilbia. Isn't it obvious?"

I looked back. Pacatus had stepped backwards towards the door but stared at us like a trapped rabbit. Jovina moved between us.

"Stay away from her!"

I couldn't have gotten closer even if I wanted to; I didn't get the chance to move anywhere of my own accord. Tiber grabbed me under the arm and thrust me down onto one of the many stools that ringed the family table. Enica protested in my defence.

"Tiber, what are you—"

"He's going to sit there and listen to what he's done." I felt very much like one of their brood having been caught tricking the baby into tightrope walking between two beds, over a sea of triangular block caltrops for added suspense. "Who are you?" Tiber added, glancing at Varro.

"The name's Varro-with-the-gimpy-leg. Not to be confused with Varro-with-one-eye and Varo-with-one-R-and-the-nasty-cough—"

"Never mind." Tiber's expression had devolved from frazzled, angry father to perplexed dormouse as he looked at Jovina and nodded his head back to Varro. "Is he one of the ones trying to hurt you?"

"I... I don't think so."

"Of course I'm not," said Varro. "I'd do anything to help this lovely woman."

Jovina could only shrug in response.

"Right," said Tiber. "I'm getting myself a beer, and then we're sorting this mess out once and for all."

I raised my eyes hopefully at at him.

"Can I have—"

"No."

<h1 style="text-align:center">18</h1>

During the interim, the room filled with even more spectators. Numbers Four and Five toddled in, accompanied by one of Jovina's twins and all three were fighting over ragdolls and animal blocks under the table. Nux sauntered over to his stool in the corner and watched over proceedings like a less-than-impartial judge. And Pacatus... Vilbia, if Varro was to be believed, was led from the room by Number Two to change.

With a cleaning cloth over her shoulder, Enica went into full mother mode and lifted my chin to inspect my forehead. She wet the corner of the cloth with her tongue and used it to dab at the drying blood around my wound.

"Oh, Titus," she murmured as she worked. "What have you got yourself into?"

I grinned, or winced. I'm not sure which.

"Don't worry. You should see the other guy."

"I saw him," Varro chipped in, raising his hand far too cheerfully from his position in the corner next to Nux. "He looked fine."

I groaned. Nux sniggered.

"Shut up, Nux."

"Right." Tiber plonked himself down at the head of the table with a mighty jug of ale and brought proceedings to a start. He pointed at me so there could be no confusion. "You are going to sit there and not say a word. Jovina came looking for me" – I opened my mouth to speak but he cut me off – "for help. Help to get you off her back. Have you any idea what has been happening here? Jovina?"

Jovina hesitated, then lowered herself onto a chair across from me. She disentangled her child from underneath the table and held it close.

"I don't know what they've told you," she said. I looked over at Tiber, who nodded permission for me to speak. I addressed him rather than her.

"Tiber, she's stolen a child—"

"No, she hasn't."

"But I've seen—"

Tiber slammed his fist onto the table. "No! You've been fed a story, and you've made what you've found fit into it. Jovina, tell him."

Jovina was quiet as she studied me, biting her lip.

"See," I said after a few moments of silence. "She—"

"Calvus," said Tiber. "Shut up."

Jovina found her voice, weak though it was. "I didn't steal Vilbia," she said. "We fled together."

"Fled? From what? Her family loves her—"

"Her family?" A hint of her customary screech of anger emerged. "Her family want to sell her to the highest bidder."

"No, they said that—"

"They said what, Calvus?" Now the hardness started to return to the edges of her eyes.

"They said she ran away because she thought, incorrectly, that they blamed her for the deaths of their kin, that you helped her, and then kept her against her will. That you were the one who would sell her off."

"And what," asked Tiber, "did they show you to support that claim?"

"I found—"

"No, never mind what you found. What did they show you?"

I thought back. All of it had been discussion. They said the shutters of her bedroom window had been smashed from the outside but it wasn't odd that they didn't show me that.

Considerable time had passed since the incident so they probably had been repaired.

"There's nothing that they could show me." I replied. "What could they?"

"So, you never thought to question the story? You never gave Jovina the benefit of the doubt?"

"Tiber, they described Jovina perfectly. I saw with my own eyes how much they missed Vilbia and loved her, and wanted her back." An image flashed in my mind of Marcella saying 'we're all actors, Titus,' at some point during our travels, but no-one could truly act that well, surely? To feign familial love where there was none?

Right?

"They told you one true thing," said Jovina. "They do blame her for the deaths of the family. And for that, they are going to make her pay." She paused for a breath as she considered her words. "Do you know how Memor is related to Marcella?"

"He's her uncle, through her mother's side."

"Yes, but he's not Vilbia's uncle."

"I know that, but he took them both in regardless. He raised the two cousins together."

Jovina baulked. "Oh wow, they've really suckered you in, haven't they?"

"I don't understand."

"You never do, Calvus." She put the baby down and stood to retrieve a small cloth bag from the kitchen bench. She returned to her seat and withdrew its contents - the Minerva statuette from her household shrine - and started turning it over in her hands, inspecting it for damage.

"When we fled the house last night," she continued, not taking her eyes off the statuette, "before Augustalis could find us, this was the only thing I took with us. Sulis has watched over us, I'm sure of it. But, if Memor is to be believed..." She sighed, and placed it upon the table. "Memor insists that Sulis Minerva fights for him. But, it can't be both ways, can it? I don't know."

"Maybe," said Tiber, "you should start by telling Calvus who Memor really is, and then we'll decide who Minerva would really be listening to."

She glanced at him, and nodded.

"Memor's father got on the wrong side of the old emperor, Domitian, and that was a dangerous place to be. The story goes that as the soldiers made their way to the Marcius estates, the boy Memor grabbed his younger sister Marcia and they fled, living on their own wits, drifting through the provinces for some time before arriving in Britannia.

"The two of them had nothing, and with nothing they had no hope. You know what gave them hope? Getting Marcia into a good marriage. A good marriage, a wealthy husband. That would give them back the lifestyle they had before, the one that was taken from them. But wealthy families want matches that increase their wealth and prestige, and Marcia could give them neither, until they found a man called Lucius Vilbius Marcellus.

"Tiber—" I turned to implore him to see reason, but to no avail.

"Just listen to her, Calvus."

I slouched on the stool with my arms crossed and glowered at her as she continued.

"Lucius Vilbius Marcellus was a wealthy man with a problem. Two problems. The Vilbius name was dwindling into extinction, and the younger of the two Vilbius brothers, Gaius, married a woman who did not sit well with the elder brother's sensibilities. An actress - that would bring shame into any family, but for one fighting for survival, it was a bad omen.

"Memor saw his opportunity and swooped. He developed a well-timed, uncanny ability to interpret the signs from the gods—"

"No," I said. "Marcella's father met Memor through the Temple. Memor already had those skills."

"Calvus," said Jovina. "If you wanted to convince someone that you could speak to the gods, would you walk straight up to them and say 'hello, I can speak to the gods'? Or would it be more convincing if that introduction came from someone trusted, someone already at the Temple?"

"And who would give them that introduction?"

She hung her head.

"Oh."

"He was so suave, so believable. He... reads people. I don't understand how, but he did it to you too. He would have taken one look at you and chosen his act. For you, he became the uncle who took his nieces under his wing. For me..." she glanced at Sulis Minerva and sighed. "Coming from northern Italia, the home of haruspicy, who was to say he didn't have those skills? I thought it would give him a chance. A hope of developing those skills. Had I known what he was truly like..."

She picked up Sulis Minerva and held her against her forehead, her eyes closed as she gathered her thoughts.

It was Varro who broke the silence next.

"Did you know that Memor's favourite play is Electra?" he asked.

"What's that got to do with anything?" I replied.

"You know that bit that prattles on about Aegisthus inspecting the entrails of a calf? There's an awfully decent amount of information there that could be recited. If you memorised that, you could convince anyone that you were a haruspex."

"Are you saying that Memor just makes it all up?"

"I'm saying that if you heard someone spouting the right-sounding words, you'd assume they knew what they were talking about."

"And, of course, you know all about Greek tragedies."

Varro shrugged. "Girl teams up with brother to murder their mother and her lover, because she had murdered their father and his lover, because he had murdered their other sister. The brother is then punished for matricide while the girl goes free to have it off with the brother's best friend. With such a whirlwind of hypocrisy, what's not to like?"

We all stared at him for a moment.

"Right, well, thank you, Varro," said Jovina as she picked up her story again. "Memor told Lucius that he and Marcia were descended from the Oceanids, specifically Doris, the mother of fifty. That would mean the blood that flows through their veins also flowed through Minerva's."

I blinked. "How—"

"Doris is Minerva's aunt."

"But that would be like, Memor's great-great-great-times-a-thousand-aunt. I think that blood might be a little diluted by now."

"Calvus, I dare you to tell that to his face."

I couldn't help it; I had to chuckle at that.

"Lucius was deeply religious," she continued. "Memor 'healed' Peregrina—"

"Peregrina?"

"Vilbia's mother. Did they not even tell you her name?"

"No," I answered, slowly.

Jovina held her tongue, but there was something on the tip of it that was struggling to get out. Something perhaps even more profane than Dio could dream up. She took a moment to regain her composure before continuing.

"Lucius invested in Memor. The more he listened to Memor, the more he believed it. And Marcia could give Lucius what he really wanted. Children, a whole brood of children, related to the gods. Lucius craved that more than wealth or political might.

"Marcella was born and the months passed. Marcia didn't live up to the prolific child-bearing reputation, but Lucius was loath to divorce her as Memor's religious power grew. At first, he was dependant on Lucius' charity. Eventually, he ran Lucius' life. Whatever he said, whatever he whispered into Lucius' ear, Lucius heeded. Memor's words, his eloquence, got him noticed, not just by Lucius but by the priests at the Temple of Sulis Minerva, until he had his tendrils well and truly throughout. Anyone who questioned him seemed to fall foul of Minerva herself until there was no question that Memor was favoured by her.

"Favoured, until tragedy struck. Memor, Marcella and Vilbia were the only survivors. Everyone, even Marcia, was gone."

Silence befell the room.

I gazed across the table at her. "So Memor took the girls in—"

"He didn't 'take them in'," she snapped. "They took him in, effectively."

"What do you mean?"

"The house they live in, everything they have, that was Lucius'. His will left the estate to Marcella but Memor challenged its legitimacy. He argued that the will was invalid, that Lucius had it prepared during a fit of lunacy, and who was going to argue with him?

"Of course, that also meant he was now the pater familias, the head of what was left of the family. Two girls, one Marcia's and one Peregrina's. Who do you think was the favourite of the pair?"

"But" – I was keen to point out – "he still took them both."

"That's not the way he saw it. He took in one - Marcella, his only true relation. He was lumbered with Vilbia. He could have adopted her, made her a part of his own true family, but no. Marcella, Marcia's daughter, was his only responsibility. He decreed that Vilbia was to blame for the illness that took the family. Vilbia was extra, a hassle. The daughter of an actress, the ones who had brought in the illness that killed them all. An unwanted and unowned girl that he had convinced the world that he had fought to save.

"And what could be done about that? He could have dashed her against the rocks and been done with it, but that would threaten his new persona that he had spent so long cooking up. But what he did have was patience. Keep the girl until she became fertile, wait for people to forget the past, then use her sale to pay for Marcella's dowry. Vilbia would not only be punished for the death of Marcia, but she would be useful. Her sale would pay for Marcella's happiness, and Memor would lose nothing."

I drew a breath as I thought.

"But, that wouldn't work."

"What do you mean?"

"People haven't forgotten. Have they, Varro?"

I looked across at the aging man, perched on a stool and rubbing his chin as he listened. He drew out his moment of attention.

"No... no, they haven't. Pay him to ask the gods for anything, and they'll provide. That's how he saved young Vilbia. That's what funds the Temple today."

"See?" I asked. "He can't sell Vilbia as you claim. His reputation depends on it"

"But what if she betrayed them? Betrayed Minerva's faith in her by healing her all those years ago?"

"What do you mean?"

"Memor is pater familias. He has absolute control over both of those girls. And what if one of them was no longer a virgin when she reached marrying age?"

I tried not to look shamefaced. I don't know if I was

successful. "That's assuming that happened by then."

"Oh, Calvus, come on. That can be arranged, and it was."

"Vilbia was raped?"

"No, but why do you think we ran?"

"They forewarned her that it was going to happen?"

"No, of course not. But—"

Her voice trailed off as the remaining members of the Tiber and Jovina clans entered the room - Numbers One and Two led the way, with Pac in behind, lugging the last twin on his hip.

Except...

Pac wasn't Pac any more.

"Figure it out, Calvus," Pac said in response to my stare.

Gone was the stained, knee-length tunic that he normally wore. In its place was an ankle-length dress in pale green, made of fine wool and belted at the waist. It's not like it was an instant transformation - Pac still looked like Pac in a dress, but, presumably no longer bound, the chest area did seem to have filled out a little.

"That's better," Enica said as she looked him over with a relaxed smile.

"Huh." I leant back against my chair. "No wonder you've never needed a shave."

Pac... Vilbia nodded. She lowered the twin to the floor to rejoin its sibling.

"Took you long enough."

Jovina stepped over to her and fussed with her short hair, the first genuine motherly act I had ever seen her perform.

"Get it now, do you, Calvus?" she asked.

"No, but I'm starting to." Too many questions were still tumbling about in my mind, and the first to make its way out of my mouth was - "How does Augustalis fit into all of this? He works for Memor?"

Jovina grimaced. "Yes. Since the early days, Augustalis has

been Memor's muscle. Didn't I tell you that anyone who questioned him seemed to fall foul of Minerva herself? Who do you think was called upon to enact Minerva's wishes?"

"But he's known where you've been for ages. I thought he was your lover?"

"Oh gods, no."

I stared at her. She stared back.

"You're going to have to spell it out," I said.

She rolled her eyes.

"Fine. Augustalis does all the unsavoury work Memor throws at him. Who do you think Memor arranged to take away Vilbia's virginity? Afterwards, Augustalis would be free to buy her as his slave. Call it a perk. But, Augustalis saw a way to make some money of his own. He was the one who tipped us off about Memor's plans. He even helped us escape, breaking the shutters on Vilbia's window so that she could climb out. Practically ripped them from the walls."

"He betrayed Memor?"

"I don't think Memor ever figured it out. Augustalis keeps on working for him. But he had tricked us. He helped her out of the window and helped us flee to Londinium. But, then he turned nasty. He started blackmailing us. He trapped us here, and... and..."

For a while, the only sound in the room was Jovina's sobbing as Vilbia hugged her. Tiber, Enica and Nux all avoided making eye contact with anyone else. Varro watched on with a placid expression and a keen eye.

It gave me time to think.

"You know what my great crime was?" I asked Jovina. "The one that everyone keeps trying to guess why I left Rome?"

She sniffed. "No."

I gave a grim, defeated smile. "I came here. That's it. My great crime was leaving Rome."

She looked at me. "That's it?"

"Well," I pulled a face. "It's not really that simple in my father's eyes. You see, Father has always had his eyes on the ultimate prize, the pinnacle of Roman greatness and splendour – an everlasting family name. He had embarked upon a quest to bring the Laelii into the awe-inspiring list that includes the Julii, the Valerii, the Claudii and the Cornelii.

"That was going to be quite a feat, instigating a flurry of work and effort lasting generations, but Father would be deified by his descendants for his vision. His bust would adorn pride of place in the future palatial family home upon the Palatine Hill, never letting his descendants rest on their laurels.

"I was meant to be the one to bring the Laelius Calvii into prominence. No expense was spared on my education, designed to thrust me up the political ladder. My marriage was arranged before I could talk, let alone voice my disapproval. The weight of two families rested on my shoulders. So, I did what any self-respecting prodigy would do.

"I left. And not just to the next town. Or the next province. I broke into Father's strongbox, took out as much money as I could safely stash about my person, and then I left for one of the farthest outposts of the empire. I left for Londinium."

Tiber sighed and shook his head. "I think you'll find your true crime wasn't coming to Londinium. It's running out on your betrothed, stealing from your family—"

"The point is, sometimes getting too hung up on what you think is the right thing for your family really just causes all sorts of heartache. Sometimes families don't do what's right by each other."

Nux laughed. "Yeah, you really screwed yours over by the sounds."

"Shut up, Nux."

The edge of a smile appeared on Jovina's face. It relaxed her muscles and her face softened ever so much.

"It all seemed so perfect, meeting and marrying Eratosthenes," she said. "If we stopped paying Augustalis, he would tell Memor where to find Vilbia and the sale would go ahead as planned. She would be his. If we tried to run, he said he would curse us and Sulis Minerva would seek our deaths. Eratosthenes was single. He had a good income from which I could siphon off Augustalis' money, and he lived in a house Vilbia's family would be unlikely to ever find.

"When he died, it was by the will of the gods. There can be no doubt about that. He slipped on the river bank fetching water and his head hit a rock. I saw it happen. But his body... I don't know what happened to his body. When he.... I washed him. I laid him on his funeral bed with flowers but nobody came to see him until Petronax came to pick him up but... I don't know if they took him... if Augustalis took him, or why. It makes no sense. But I don't know how I am going to placate our gods without him."

"Not your gods," Tiber grunted. "Just their representatives."

"But then," said Jovina, "Memor found you. They found you, Calvus, and now Augustalis is about to lose his income, so he's gone back to the original plan. He's trying to find her, and when he does, he'll drag her to Memor and the sale will be done."

"But how does Augustalis know what's happening?" I asked.

"Oh, I can answer that," Varro-with-the-gimpy-leg piped in. "Remember I said Memor met with Augustalis? They mentioned a low-life, wannabe boot-licker trying his luck at playing an influential bastard. That sounds like you, right?"

I blinked. "Thanks, I think, Varro."

Varro laughed. "You thought they were looking for you, didn't you? They don't give a crap about you. Not unless they find out about—"

"Yes, thank you, Varro."

"All their money's on Augustalis finding Vilbia."

"He's certainly giving it a good try. He's smashed up my house. Oh" – I ran a hand over my face – "the workshop…"

"What about the workshop?" Tiber asked.

"Ah, well… good news!"

"What?"

"We now own Londinium's largest supply of cullet to shape into a brand new range of products."

Tiber stared at me. When he did react, he shifted his gaze across to Jovina.

"Jovina?" he asked.

"Yes?"

"We could kill Calvus now, and blame it on Memor if you like."

"Sounds good to me."

"No, wait," I stammered, thinking fast. "I can fix this."

After some consideration, the general consensus of the room was that I would do everything to put things right while they all sat tight and ate snacks.

19

We all spent the night at Tiber and Enica's. Room was made for Jovina, Vilbia and Varro by shuffling Tiber's brood around - Number One and Number Two moved into Number Three and Number Four's beds, and so forth down the line until Number Four and Number Five clambered into Tiber and Enica's bed with them. Jovina's twins shared Nux's stretcher. Nux got a borrowed mattress from the neighbours.

And me?

I got a blanket on the floor.

That seemed understandable in the circumstances.

I spread my blanket out in the silent dining room and sat down, a single candle fighting back the dark. Maybe Tiber had been right, way back however long ago. Maybe I should have just got stuck into good, honest, physical work and bore the tedium with grace. The simple life. Vilbia would still be safe in hiding, Memor would have no idea where she was and her pending sale to Augustalis would not be an imminent threat.

But, would that really have been better?

I stood by my actions. I tried to help a bereaved family, tried to find a missing cousin whom I believed was loved, and tried to solve a murder. Should I really have just stood back and watched all this stuff unfold around me? I had brought matters to a head, but could Vilbia really have remained in hiding indefinitely?

Hades, having a conscience makes life complicated.

A shuffling sound near the door alerted me to the fact I was no longer alone. Vilbia stepped into the room and sat beside me. Outside, a nightingale trilled and gurgled into the dark.

"I'm sorry I tried to make you dig barley trenches," I said.

She chuckled. "That was never going to happen."

"Yeah, I know."

"I'm sorry Augustalis smashed up your house."

"That's okay." I thought on that for a moment. "Why did he do that? He knows where you live."

In the scant light, I could not see her face clearly, but I detected a hint of humour in her voice. "Did you know our key opens your door?"

"Ah, what answer can I give to that, that doesn't make me look bad?"

"It's all right, I'm pretty certain you've searched our house by now."

"Then yes, I do know our locks have the same key."

"So...?"

"So?"

"So, Augustalis has been visiting us for a long time now. Where do you think I hide?"

"No. If you were in my house, I'd know."

"With all that beer you drink, you're lucky it's just me. You snore, you know."

"I..." I gave a defeated chuckle. "Guess I'd better stay awake tonight for everyone's benefit."

"For sure. The walls would quiver."

"I'm not that bad—" She threw me a sideways glance. I sighed. "All right, so you'd hide from Augustalis using my foundation-shaking caterwauling—"

"Not caterwauling. More of a bellow."

"...as a cover. But there's something else. Something I don't think even Jovina knows. What did you take from Memor?"

She cocked her head to the side, the perplexity she felt evident in her voice.

"What do you mean, 'what did I take'?"

"You've been running from Memor for what, two years now?"

"Give or take."

"Well, if he'd just wanted to sell you to pay for Marcella's dowry, why is he still bothering to look for you?" I sensed her understanding of my meaning but I continued anyway. "I saw the inside of that house, money is of no consequence. So, why hasn't he given up and cut his losses?"

"I suppose I did take something from him," she said with a hint of pride in her voice. "I took away his ability to be the biggest fish."

"What do you mean?"

"Jovina and I are the only people to disobey Uncle Memor and get away with it. Sort of," she said. "Everybody else has ended up... well, Augustalis enjoys himself. But we haven't, and I bet all of Aquae Sulis knows that."

"You've undermined his authority."

"If that's how you want to put it."

"With you and Jovina still at large, people may start to question whether he's still Minerva's favourite. His grip over the Temple will slip. He has to find you so that his power remains unquestioned."

"I hope it keeps him up at night."

We sat in companionable silence for a time, listening to the faint noises of the sleeping household. Now that I knew, now that I was looking, Pac... Vilbia did bear some resemblance to Marcella, but she was younger and more gaunt. On the cusp of womanhood but not yet physically there. If I were ever to become a proper informer, I'd have to practice my observation skills.

"What?" she asked as she sensed my inspection of her silhouette.

"Nothing. Just thinking. You know, I've got some of your dolls stashed away at my place. When it's safe to go back, I'll fetch them for you."

"Dolls? What dolls?"

"Little wooden people, about so tall—" I spaced my fingers apart to demonstrate.

"I don't own any dolls. Jovina and I took nothing with us, nothing that could be recognised. Even her Sulis statue isn't her original one. She bought it at a market the day after she married Eratosthenes."

I cocked my head. "Are you sure? I found one in your shed, and the rest... well, never mind where the rest were." I had decided not to mention the cell in the cliff-face yet, and whatever Eratosthenes might have been planning. I had realised that had Jovina been in on the whole affair, she would have visited the cell after Eratosthenes' death and Nonnus would have known what was happening. "But I'm sure the dolls are yours."

She shook her head. "Not mine. We were never allowed in the shed, anyway. That was Eratosthenes'. He was pretty adamant about it."

"Not even Jovina?"

She shook her head and yawned. The thoughts that were keeping her awake were at last succumbing to exhaustion and she stood to go back to bed, but she looked back at me.

"You want to ask me about Marcella?"

I sighed.

"Did she know? What Memor was planning?"

Vilbia nodded. "Of course. She looked forward to it more than anything else. Good night, Calvus."

"'Night, Pac."

"Vilbia."

"Whatever."

She smiled and took two steps towards the door before turning back to me.

"Don't believe whatever Marcella tells you. She lies. Oh, and you're not her first."

"But—"

"I know my cousin. I know how she gets her way. Tell you what, though. If Memor knows, he's ignoring the fact. Talk about double-standards."

She padded out of the room.

I didn't have a plan for what to do next.

When I had arrived back in Londinium, I had planned to search Jovina's house for clues and ended up in terror of rectal homicide.

Then, I planned to convince Tiber of her murderous intent through sheer weight of evidence but instead ended up being chased out of an underground cell by a rampaging quarryman.

Finally, as I planned a safe haven at the workshop, I was beset upon by Marcella's wiles before being pummelled by Augustalis.

Having a plan was going to kill me.

"Wait up," Varro-with-the-gimpy-leg called out after me as I let myself out the front and into the morning light. "I'm coming with you."

"Why?"

"This is the most fun I've had in years, I'm not missing out on a moment of it. Where are we going?"

I stopped walking and thought.

"Petronax," I said after a moment. I nodded. "Yep. That feels right."

Eratosthenes was at the centre of some pretty big unanswered questions. Eratosthenes, his nefarious cell, and his disappearing corpse.

Once across the river, Varro acted as a scout to make sure the temple courtyard was clear of anyone professing to be a part of Minerva's inner circle. With no sign of Memor, Marcella or

Augustalis, we introduced ourselves to the nearest official as two prospective members of the Funeral Club and requested to meet with Petronax, but with no luck - the bastard wasn't there.

"I'm beginning to think he runs this entire place by delegation," I said to the frazzled little cleric but he wouldn't be drawn in.

"He's a busy man." He bustled away and left us standing alone in the open courtyard. Varro pursed his lips and looked at me.

"So, what's the plan now?"

"No plan. Only instinct and intuition today. Today, we follow whatever I feel in my gut, not my mind."

"Okay, and what's this savvy stomach of yours telling you now?"

I looked around. The altar was tinged dark - not wet, but dark and certainly not from an intense incense-burning session. Something else had happened here yesterday after I had left, something that had demanded the attention of the visiting haruspex, which meant...

"Spit roast."

"That's not an instinct," replied Varro. "That's an addiction."

"No, I mean they had one here, yesterday. The boys who run it should be around here some place."

I led him around the back and sure enough, the cellar door was open. Inside were my two chaste-faced chefs, tending to three carcasses hanging from hooks in the ceiling: a ram, a pig and a bull.

"Hi there, boys," I called out and they jumped. Before they could start throwing their gutting knives at us, the elder of the pair thankfully experienced that moment of recognition.

"Oh! Where was you yesterday? Thought you'd be a regular," he said.

"Yeah, sorry. Couldn't make it. Got anything left over? My friend here would love to try some."

"Yeah, but it's not for you. Been claimed by Petronax himself."

"Really? We were told he wasn't here."

"'Course he's not." The boy smirked at my ignorance and jerked his head towards the other lad. "Ajax here is to run it over to him for his lunch."

"Oh?" Things were looking up. "Well, maybe we can save you the trip. Give it to us, and we'll run it over for you. Just tell us where to go."

They leapt at the chance to abscond from their duties. They handed over a significant chunk of a roasted pork leg, instructed us to visit a bakery along the way to pick up the side-dish, and gave us clear and precise directions to Petronax' house.

"Varro," I said as we made our way back to the bridge, our mouths full with the meat that Petronax would never see. "Do you think Minerva is still on our side after all?"

"Hmm..." He paused to pick at a bit of gristle in his teeth. He examined the culprit on the end of his finger, shrugged, and popped it back in. "Those kids asked us to transport goods, which we've then stolen. I think Mercury, god of messengers, merchants and thieves, has taken a shine to you."

"Well, whoever it is, I approve of their work."

We arrived at a tidy but compact wooden house, two streets back from the main road leading towards the Forum. A slave answered the door. Well, I say answered, but he only cracked it open enough to tell us that Petronax was not receiving visitors today. We explained that we had been sent by the Temple on an urgent matter, and the door closed in our faces.

Another knock on the door simply would not do. The matter called for incessant hammering. Eventually the door cracked open again, this time wide enough for Petronax's beaked nose to peek through as he peered out.

"Go away. I'm busy."

He tried to close the door but I had slipped the toe of my boot into the gap. Bet he didn't see that coming. The obvious solution would be to open the door further, build up momentum and smash it against my foot but he hesitated. "Please move."

"It's me, Calvus. I'm here to get my mask made up," I told him. "My funerary mask, you know, that you were going to make for me as part of my new funeral insurance plan a few weeks ago? I realised I never came back. So rude of me. Do you remember?"

Petronax grunted. "No. Yes, well, it will have to wait until another time." He put his weight against the door to squeeze my foot out.

"What's going on, Pet?" I asked.

He winced, either from me calling him 'Pet' or from the aroma now wafting out through the door gap.

It was truly rancid.

"Oh gods!" I wrapped my elbow across my face.

"Go away!"

"What is that?" I pushed harder. He pushed back, so Varro and I put our shoulders to the door and rammed it open with brute force.

Behind Petronax, visible through the short corridor beyond the entrance and in a small, paved courtyard beyond, was Eratosthenes.

***

Eratosthenes was very much not alive.

Eratosthenes was laid out on a table in the sun, his chest cavity open and his skin shrivelled and grey.

"Dis!" I turned from the door and retched, but Petronax no longer fought to get us out.

"It's what he wanted," he said weakly. "But it's not working. I don't understand why it's not working."

Varro-with-the-gimpy-leg was not in the least perturbed. Seeing a partially decomposed cadaver seemed to remind him of his hey-day in the legions as he moved inside. He appeared to be inspecting the thing with a morbid nostalgia.

"Ha! Your friend's Egyptian?"

"So?" I spluttered.

"So, what do well-to-do Egyptians do when they die?"

"What in Hades?" I glared at Petronax. "*That's* the service he requested of you?"

All the fight had gone from him. All the fight, life, colour and vitality of being, so that his face resembled the mummy that he was attempting to make.

"I thought I could do it. I thought... but it's not..."

"Does Jovina know?"

"Jovina?"

"His wife."

"Oh. No. He couldn't afford to get them both done. She isn't meant to find out. She was meant to think he was buried but, but..."

"But she saw the body had been switched."

"Yes. Don't tell her. He felt bad that he couldn't give her eternal life, but the cost is too great. We kept him in the cellar while we ran the decoy funeral. I was to place him in his tomb, it's all organised, but it's not working. The natron..."

"Natron?"

"Soda. It dries the body out so that it can be wrapped."

"You're the one who brought in all that stuff? That Dio sold to Tiber?"

"No, no, Eratosthenes had it all organised, he had it all

worked out, the natron, the tools, the little wooden ushabti dolls to serve him in death. But he died. He died too soon, his instructions were incomplete. I fetched what was needed, but there was so much, surely it would not take all that natron? All those tools? It was excessive. I took what I thought I would need."

Petronax had botched it. I had no doubt that Eratosthenes had calculated it all with absolute precision; he was a man who made lists like his life depended upon it, after all. But Petronax had doubted him, had tried to save a few coins, and now...

I tried to look back at the body, being stuffed with linen to maintain its shape, but I couldn't bring myself to do it. Here was someone who really was having his brains removed with a spoon; I know that, because Varro was holding said spoon up to his face, inspecting it with fascination. I didn't need to have that image appearing in my waking nightmares any more than necessary. I turned on my heal and we left.

20

"No wonder we had no money," was all Jovina could say to break the stunned silence. She slumped on a stool in Tiber's kitchen as Vilbia held her hand.

We had told her. Of course we had. She had been thinking this whole time that Augustalis or Memor had taken the body as some sort of macabre threat. The truth was much weirder. The only mummy in Britannia.

The surreal atmosphere that our story had caused was more than I could bear. I retreated to the carpenter's storage and sat alone with my thoughts. Sweet, earthy dust motes bobbed and floated in the intermittent shafts of light, dancing to the score of the carpenter's saw next door and the higher-pitched snippets of conversation from within the house.

"...but mummification, for Minerva's sake..."

"...a spoon up the nose? How..."

"...his own religion, you say?"

I was not given long to sit in melancholy before the step-thunk of Varro's gait interrupted my thoughts.

"Come on," he said, passing me without pausing. "There's someone you need to meet."

"Meet?" I slid off the stack of beams that had served as my seat and trailed after him. "Who do you know in Londinium?"

"No-one," he said as we emerged onto the street. "It's someone I brought with me. Now, point me in the direction of the docks. We've been staying at a lovely little place down there. And on the way, you can tell me of this new religion of yours that Nux has been describing."

I shook my head. "Well, you can tell Nux his worries about that are no more. I don't think it's ever going to happen."

"Nonsense. It has to survive, at least another week. After that, you can do what you want with it."

"What are you talking about?"

But he refused to say another word, not until we got to this quaint accommodation of his.

Once at the docks, Varro had his bearings back and led me past a string of moored boats. I spotted Dio's dinghy amongst them, which he had optimistically named 'Fish Killer' in the hopes that his riverine escapades would prove productive. I don't know if the name was apt in keeping with his abilities with a line and a hook, but I was certain that, should he ever convince me to join him, he would have to have a renaming ceremony, with the boat henceforth to be known as 'Fish Non-fatal'.

We swung a left down a laneway and I kept my hopes up, but I was getting the distinct impression that Varro, a man who was engrossed by a partially dissected corpse, might have a different definition of 'quaint' than me. Back in the day, when I had fled my tutor's 'Economy of the Grain Dole' lesson and had taken an impromptu holiday to the port of Ostia with money pinched from Father's strongbox, I had stayed at a 'quaint' riverside guest-house by the Grandi Horrea, the massive grain warehouses built by the Emperor Claudius to feed a city. Watching from my accommodation's ivy-covered balconies, I had learnt more about shipping than I ever would from a monotone lecture. I saw the high-hulled corbitae coming into dock under a headsail, which my tutor would no doubt be able to describe in precise nautical terms.

He would not have described the salty haze, the shouts of dockworkers manoeuvring laden carts with axles threatening to break, the black-headed gulls harassing the fishing boats, nor the buskers who seemed to have never handled a musical instrument in their lives, with their broken-stringed lute and mis-timed cymbals. They were hoping to be tossed the change from the takeaway stall nearby, whose proprietor was dishing out cooked molluscs with a definite nervous twitch developing in her left eye.

That was my idea of a riverside accommodation with character.

The accommodation that Varro and his friend had found did not live up to that expectation, but, to be fair, it could have been worse. There was no grand view of imperial weight, and it was seedy, but only in the sense that two-leaved shoots emerged from cracks in the floor, anticipating a great and full life before being squished underfoot.

A man sat in the corner of the common room, face hidden, as men always do in places such as this. Part of me expected Memor or Augustalis to throw off the cloak, dagger in hand, screeching in joy at the double-cross, but the wild hair and drawn face that glared up as Varro introduced us was different.

"Calvus, this is Amatus. Amatus, this is Calvus." Varro lowered himself onto the stool opposite. "Welcome to the first clandestine meeting of the Cult of... what's your god's name?"

"Vitrumesh."

"The Cult of Vitrumesh, membership: three." Varro waved a hand at the proprietor as he slunk by and ordered whatever was available in the pantry for lunch. I don't know how he could be hungry. I certainly wasn't, and I doubted I ever would be again.

I cleared my throat and glanced at Amatus. I had also lost my appetite for the whole 'cult' idea. "He's not real, you know," I said, directing the comment back to Varro.

"Vitrumesh? Good, even better. Now, to business. You seem intent on not planning anything any more, but you're going to need one. A plan, that is. Memor and Augustalis are powerful and rich. They'll want you dead by the end of all of this and they know where you live."

"Oh, great."

Varro paused as the owner returned. He thunked down a plate of cold sausages on the table between us. They were overcooked - the skin had thickened and shrivelled, and it would not have been a stretch of the imagination to compare them with another shrivelled hunk of meat we had already seen this morning. Varro grabbed one and took to it with passion.

"Excellent," he said. If the image of Eratosthenes didn't put him off his food, then neither Amatus nor I staring at him while he gnawed away was going to faze him in the slightest. I didn't know if Varro was going to explain Amatus to me, but he seemed content to let us sit in awkward silence while he ate.

"Now," he said with his mouth full, pointing at me with the remains of the sausage in his hand. "Option one is, you pretend that you don't know that they're all a bunch of jerks and hand Vilbia over to them."

"Not going to happen."

"Good."

"What's option two?"

"Option two is, you pretend you don't know they're all a bunch of jerks and buy yourself time to pack up and flee the province."

I blinked. "And number three?"

"Option three is, you pretend you don't know that they're all a bunch of jerks, and we turn their game against them. Whichever way, you've got to do some pretty convincing acting."

I looked at Amatus, who was glaring at Varro with a look of death in his eyes. As Amatus had yet to even acknowledge my presence, let alone speak, I directed my question to Varro.

"So, option three is where Amatus comes into it?"

Varro nodded. "Amatus here has a gripe of his own to take up with Memor. If you work together, you might just pull this off."

I rubbed the bridge of my nose. "I think you'd better explain what your plan is, then."

***

I had my doubts about Varro's plan, so I did what I thought best.

I told Tiber.

He gazed at me as he leant his backside against his kitchen bench, arms crossed. "You're going to host a fake ceremony to put the fear of a false god into them, to convince them to leave us all alone on pain of divine retribution?"

"Yes."

He thought on that for moment.

"Good."

"Come again?"

He picked up a small bowl of pistachios from the bench and joined me at the table, putting it between us to share.

"They've done it to enough people," he said. "It's time they experienced that for themselves." He regarded my puzzled expression. "What?"

I shook my head. "I guess I'm just confused. Why are you okay with this? Memor represents a real goddess."

"I reckon that if Minerva has something to say about the matter, she's powerful enough to send us a sign."

"You'd have to ask Memor about that."

"Just because Memor tells people she's okay with what he does, doesn't mean that she is."

We all pitched in to devise the plan of action. I was sold on planning again - it seemed safer to plan in numbers and if the gods disapproved, maybe the lightning bolt wouldn't hit me first and I'd have time to duck. In a way, for all of us, the planning of phoney divine retribution on those who would do the same was quite a cathartic experience.

Step one was my least favourite by far: cleaning up the workshop. Nux leered at me as he handed me the broom, knowing full well that finally I would have to use it. He took the shop while I tackled the storeroom.

As he ran his eye over my efforts, I leant on the broom and awaited his judgement.

"Maybe stick with religion-building," he said. "Cleaning isn't your calling in life."

"Finally, he gets it."

"Shut up, Calvus."

"Shut up, Nux."

Step two - convincing Memor that Vitrumesh was a real and powerful god with loyal followers. This was a fun step, because it involved Petronax.

"Can't you just leave me alone?" he whined, with my foot once again in his doorway and Varro by my side.

"Nope."

The smell lingered but Eratosthenes was no longer visible. It had now been three days since our last run-in - cleaning had only taken one of those days, but as for the other two days, well, I'll get to that in a moment. During the period in which we had left him in peace, Petronax had returned Eratosthenes to the natron, convinced that the process needed more time, not more supplies.

I dangled a necklace in front of Petronax's face.

"We need you to wear this around for the next week or two."

He squinted at it.

"What is it?"

What it was, was the partial result of two days' work by the furnaces - glass beads in alternating blue and red. Hanging from the centre was a round glass amulet, streaked red and yellow, and bearing the glimmering Mark of Vitrumesh.

Minerva had the owl.

Eratosthenes had been fond of Horus' eye as a protective sign to ward off evil.

Many Romans picked a body part that was much lower, wearing the divine phallus around their necks for protection. You can tell it's divine because it's got little wings and everything.

The Mark of Vitrumesh was...

Well...

It was supposed to be a snake wrapped around a glass of beer. It was the best approximation of that, that Number One could carve in the time, so rather than receive an answer to his question, all Petronax got in response was—

"Just wear it around, okay?"

"Why should I?"

"Varro," I said, turning to grin at my accomplice. Varro looked at me with an innocent, and yet oh-so curious expression. "Which do you think the population of Londinium would hate more? That the founder of the Vejovis and Libitina Funeral Club botches burials and leaves corpses rotting in the sun, or that the head priest of the Temple of Mars Camulus and the Imperial Cult cheats when he holds sacrificial spit roast parties?"

"You wouldn't dare," Petronax growled.

"Try me."

He tried to stare me down, his knuckles turning white as he clutched the oak door frame. I gazed back at his mismatched eyes with fascination.

"Fine," he said at last, snatching the piece from my fingers. "And then you'll leave me alone?"

"Well, there's one more thing," I replied. "You've got two boys in that cellar of yours. I'll need them for a week or so too."

"Why?"

I returned my attention to Varro. "You know, it's hard to work out. A botched burial only affects one person, but that's a great big afterlife no-no. The spit roast is really only one illegitimate luncheon, but there's so many stomachs to be turned—"

"Take them."

"Thank you. We appreciate your assistance."

There was a good reason why we needed the two boys. Petronax would not be the only person wearing the Mark of Vitrumesh. We had taken the template that Number One had made and pushed it into hard-packed sand. A fast but single-use mould that we could reform over and over. The number of amulets we could churn out was only limited by time.

Fifty trinkets had been drizzled into existence in molten glass, and now we needed someone to sell them far and wide.

No, not far and wide. The opposite to that, actually.

We needed someone to sell them to anyone that Memor might cross paths with over the course of a few days, and that's where the two boys came in. We loaded them up with trays and sent them out to hock necklaces in strategically-selected locales. The bathhouse down the road from Memor's mansio. The takeaway selling lentil porridge and spicy mushy peas. And, in a little market stall nearby to the classiest of the public latrines.

The Mark of Vitrumesh was southern Londinium's latest hot fashion accessory.

While we worked away at the furnaces, and Jovina, Vilbia and Enica worked away at Tiber's house stitching up our sacred garb, Varro took up position out the front of the shop, posing as a disabled beggar. He had worked out an elaborate routine of shrieking like a madman should Augustalis reappear, but we remained undisturbed throughout.

Each lunch time, I emerged from the shop and split a bread roll and chunks of cheese and cold meat with him, as if taking pity on the poor sod. I leant on the door-frame and watched him eat. No-one paid us any attention.

"Who is Amatus?" I asked.

"A friend."

"But who is he, really? Why does he have a problem with Memor?"

"You don't need to worry about that."

"That makes me worry more."

"Trust me, it's enough to know that he will come through for us on the day."

Amatus was to pose as my assistant during the official proceedings. Until now, he had barely spoken three words to us, and so had not been assigned a job of his own. He seemed content with that, taking long walks and brooding by the docks.

"Jovina knows him," Varro pointed out. "She trusts him."

"Jovina vaguely remembers his face."

"There you go, she remembers him. It'll be fine." He glanced around but the street was quiet. "Now, how are you going on the location?"

I gnawed on my bread end, pulling my second-to-last bite away; just the right mix of chewy inside and crunchy crust. The sun was about two hours from setting. It was time.

"I need to go see a man about a dog."

Or, more specifically, a merchant about a stage. With Tiber's blessing, I left them to it and made my way to the docks.

***

Dio came through for us. He always does. By nightfall, we had a premises promised for the inaugural Temple of Vitrumesh (a vacant warehouse, river adjacent), a cast of worshippers (the Tarraconensis Troupe, in their greatest performance of the season), and more besides - Dio knew a man, who knew a man, who could get us a curved augur's staff for taking auspices to complete the scene.

In return for Dio's efforts, we signed away Jovina's house to him. Whatever the outcome of the night, she had neither need nor desire to return there. Where they would go was a mystery yet to be solved, but that house had been a prison from which they could not escape Augustalis' torment. Besides, Dio rather fancied adding "landlord" to his list of socially-questionable job descriptions.

Oh, and the only other caveat to the deal was that I could not ask any questions as to why he had entered the room rubbing something viscous, dark and red-tinged off his hands with a rag.

That seemed a fair deal under the circumstances.

The night before I was to approach Memor, we rehearsed everything in Tiber's kitchen. Every question, every possible outcome that we could predict, the others threw my way until I knew the responses by heart. We sent a message to Memor, telling him I had some promising news, and that was that.

It was all up to me now.

I said a silent prayer to Vitrumesh as I departed Tiber's house mid-morning. I knew he was fake, but he still owed us one for bringing him into existence in the first place.

<h1 style="text-align:center">21</h1>

The reply I received to my message was succinct to say the least:

Temple of Mars Camulus and the Imperial Cult. Fourth hour after sunrise.

Honestly, there's not much more Memor could have said in response to my own request for a meeting. The message I had sent was deliberately innocuous:

I have news. Let's meet. Your place or mine?

No detail, no guff. Just enough mystery to leave them guessing.

When I arrived, with Memor's message clutched in my hand as evidence that I had indeed been summoned, I was led away from the courtyard and behind the Temple to where Memor awaited me. This was indeed to prove fortunate, although I knew Memor's intent was to intimidate me. Away from prying eyes? Assuming that, by now, I knew Augustalis was out to get me, either for bedding Marcella or for hiding Vilbia, or probably both?

Most men would be quivering in their sandals to have been led away from the safety offered by a busy thoroughfare, especially as I felt members of Memor's entourage join us from behind.

But I am not most men.

I knew about the meat cellar. And that gave me the advantage. Or at least the confidence to believe I had the advantage.

Memor had made himself comfortable. He awaited me upon a curved bench brought forth from elsewhere, underneath a portable awning for shade, with a wine cup in his hand. He would not lower himself by standing while he waited and if this was to be my end, he would watch on in luxury.

It was a premium-class theatre seat and it was time for the show.

"Haruspex Memor," I said, my face beaming with delight to see him. "You are a hard man to pin down. I tried to visit you last week."

"So I heard," he replied. "And how was my niece?"

"Expensive and eager," I replied. His eyes narrowed. "The shops of Londinium must be better than those of Aquae Sulis. But, you'll be pleased to know that I have news of your other niece."

"Will I? I do hope so, Calvus."

I felt his buddies behind me move a little closer.

"I believe—"

I didn't get the chance to say anything else before the first thug noticed our small surprise.

Now, I say small...

"Holy mother of Dis!"

The entourage scattered to the sounds of yelps and howls. Memor, with considerable difficulty, hauled his legs upon the bench, and balanced his considerable frame with knees tucked under his chin (or as close as they could get), lest any part of his body should touch the ground.

I stood perfectly still. That was the one thing I had learned in my twenty-minute introductory course to 'Obscenely Large African Python Handling', courtesy of the Tarraconensis Troupe's animal handler. His gem, the jewel in the crown of the troupe's repertoire, now slithered between Memor and me, as if this was the role he was born to play.

Draco was not your average snake. If Tiber and I lay down, head to toe, Draco would still have another foot of length on us and the body weight to match - it took two adults to carry his chestnut-blotched body.

"But, don't worry," his handler had cheerfully informed me. "He's not poisonous and he very rarely kills people. We just use him when we're re-enacting the mating of Echidna the snake woman and Typhon the serpentine giant."

I didn't ask how that was performed.

"My lord, Vitrumesh!" I bowed my head with the appearance of reverence, but in reality to hide the grin that I was struggling to keep from my face. Having spent several hours in the chill of the cellar, accompanied by his handler and the two over-excited and awe-struck spit-roast boys who had helped to smuggle them in during the small hours of the morning, Draco was sluggish and placid. He glided through the chaos unfazed, his eyes upon the sunlit courtyard beyond. We hadn't really thought about what would happen should he make his way into the less-than-adoring public, but luckily we didn't have to - the scent of a strategic chicken carcass in the bushes by the river drew him away to be reclaimed by awaiting assistants.

"Vitrumesh?" Memor's yellowing eyes darted from the snake to myself.

"It is a sign, Haruspex," I said as I pulled out my own Mark of Vitrumesh necklace from beneath my tunic and kissed it. I was pleased to note Memor's gaze had fixed itself upon the amulet. "As sure as any other. Vitrumesh has sent us an omen. He has sent us the offspring of Oomes, the great serpent. Our meeting here is not auspicious. We must seek Vitrumesh's blessing before proceeding further."

"Blessing... how?"

"I must prepare." I hurried away, prattling off lists of religious paraphernalia and sacred texts to myself.

"Calvus, wait!"

I spun to face him but did not stop, walking backwards as I spoke.

"An hour after sunset. Come alone. Across the bridge, first right, then the third right after that. You'll know it when you see it."

"Calvus!"

But I was gone.

***

"What are you doing?"

"Juice," was all Amatus would reply.

He squatted, hunched over a mortar and pestle, squishing berries into oblivion with a singular focus. I paced Dio's shack, to which we had added as many decorations as we could cram in, to transform it into a temporary abode fit for Vitrumesh.

The building consisted of one largish room, five good paces wide by about fifteen, with the back divided off behind free-standing partitions to create a smaller office. Dio normally reserved the building for overflow stock, or for deliveries that were too hot to have associated with his main place of business. It seemed either business was slow or Dio was unusually well-behaved lately, as the place was practically bare. Anything that was left, we piled behind the partition.

Access was provided in one of three ways - the main doorway onto the street (via a small, overgrown front yard), the large delivery doors off to the left that opened out onto the newly-dedicated 'Dock of Vitrumesh', or via the small back door past the partition. It was from there that Draco was destined to appear in his encore performance, the ultimate bad omen, a sign that the gods forbade Vilbia to return to Memor's clutches.

In the centre of the room, a table had been set as an altar and upon it sat our masterpiece.

Well, Tiber's masterpiece.

He had spent considerable time sorting our smashed stock by

197

colour, before melting it down and drawing out large canes of recycled glass. These he cut into smaller pellets, which he arranged in a pattern before remelting and squishing them to form a solid slab. While soft, the slab was eased over a mould to form a deep bowl, more colourful and mysterious than any I had ever seen. To the untrained eye, this solid piece with swirls and spirals of rainbows could only have come forth from divine creation.

The Bowl of Vitrumesh.

In hindsight, I should not have been the one to name the sacred items of our dreamed-up deity. My imagination had run out, long ago. Without help, the mighty Vitrumesh's titles would have been "Something of the Something. Keeper of the Something. Something of the Something Something."

It was pointed out by numerous self-appointed editors of the first draft of my sacred script that this would probably raise a few sceptical eyebrows amongst my congregation. I pointed out that it added to the mystery and that when a person is fully initiated, they would get to learn what the somethings are, but no-one went for that.

In any case, it was into the Bowl of Vitrumesh that Amatus now poured the latest batch of his nectar.

"Just let him do his thing," Varro said from his leaning post, bundled up in an obnoxiously large cloak against the cool evening air. "He's traversed half the woodlands within half a day's hike from here, scouting for ingredients. Just make sure Memor drinks that stuff first."

"Why?"

"It'll get him in the mood."

The three of us, dressed in our costumes, awaited Memor's arrival - me in loose-fitting trousers tucked into my boots and a light, long jacket over my tunic. Amatus was dressed much the same, with the addition of a hood to hide his face in the dark, lest

Memor recognise him. The design was the best approximation of Parthian fashion that my limited attention-span could remember from the tales of Trajan's conquest, combined with what a budget built from the small change under Tiber's bed could afford in fabric at the markets. Enica had been promised the clothing afterwards, to re-cut into a range of children's clothes.

In a stroke of luck, the six actors of the Tarraconensis Troupe came pre-dressed in costume. Apparently, their retelling of the overrunning of the Parthian city of Ctesiphon by Trajan's Roman troops, five-ish years ago, was a popular story in the theatre circuit, in as far as six actors and an unrelated snake dancer could re-enact of the slaying of thousands.

Varro spun a coin over and over on a bench nearby, the clatter-clink, clatter-clink giving me a nervous twitch.

"Must you?"

"Must I what?"

Clatter-clink.

Clatter-clink.

"Never mind."

...

Clatter-clink.

"Well," said Varro as he scooped up his coin and the chipped glass tumbler we had provided. "Best be taking up position."

The sun had dipped below the horizon and the actors went to work lighting the scattered lanterns and pots of incense. There was no way that we had the money for frankincense, so instead we burned pots of rosemary leaves, sourced from a bush that was overhanging someone's front fence, which we had found along the way.

Varro's job was to do what he did best - pose as a beggar outside and keep a look out. I watched as he hobbled towards the door. I could have sworn that his limp had spread to his other leg - no longer just lurching to the left, it appeared his right leg was stiffening as well. It had been some time since his last visit to Minerva's healing baths, perhaps it was overdue.

"You remember what to do?" I asked.

He held up his glass with the coin inside, shaking it as he walked. The coin clattered and jingled with some volume - our cue to take our positions.

"Let's see if we can take the bastard for a coin or two before he comes in."

22

The clatter of metal on glass and the gruff "spare some coins?" came all too soon and all thoughts of 'maybe we should have rehearsed' became too late to act upon. We scampered to our places.

"Calvus!" Memor's voice came from the doorway a moment before his bulk filled the frame. "'You'll know it when you see it', my backside—"

"Shush," I hushed him from before the altar. No-one had shushed Memor in quite some time and the silence that followed had the distinct sensation of being 'stunned' rather than 'reverent'. No matter. I hurried over to him and placed a Mark of Vitrumesh around his neck.

"You are alone?" I asked, surprised and relieved.

"You said—"

"Quietly!"

"You said," he whispered, "to come alone."

I noted that technically he had not answered my question, but we had something here that should keep proceedings civil - too many witnesses. I moved to walk back inside into the air now heavy with the scent of the Incense of Vitrumesh. Maybe one pot would have been enough. Six billowing forth their sweet, woody smoke seemed to be overkill.

"Good—"

"Hello, Titus."

A feminine voice. My heart leapt into my throat as I turned back towards the door.

No.

"Marcella..."

Memor raised an eyebrow as Marcella stepped out from

behind him with a sheepish grin.

"You never said it was a male-only ceremony," Memor pointed out.

"I...ah..."

"This way," came Amatus' voice behind me, keeping us on track. Memor nodded once and stepped around me into the building as I stared at Marcella.

"I hope you don't mind," she said.

"You're not supposed to be here. Not for this—"

I stopped speaking as she reached under the neckline of her stola and pulled out a Mark of Vitrumesh. The woman who loved to shop had visited a market stall nearby to the classiest of the public latrines.

She winked.

"I'm sure Vitrumesh won't mind," she said. She looked down at it as she spoke. "Uncle Lucius said you were wearing one this morning, at the Temple. And here was me, thinking it was just some funny little local good-luck trinket." She, too, sidestepped around me and moved up next to Memor. Gripping the door frame, I peered into the dark outside. I couldn't make out Varro's face, only his hunched, squatting form, melding into the bushes.

Behind me, the Tarraconensis Troupe took up a chant, three musical notes repeated over and over. I drew a breath and turned back inside.

"Oh, mighty Vitrumesh," I intoned as I stepped slowly towards the altar and the chant dwindled into silence. "Slayer of Oomes. Keeper of the Mash. He of the Chug and the Glass. We remove ourselves from our usual routines of life to hear your voice tonight."

As I approached, the congregation parted to let me through. I reached the altar, bowed to it, straightened and turned to face my worshippers.

"Tonight—"

A bell chimed behind me. I turned to see Amatus raise a ladle above his head, high above with arms straight, as if it were a symbol of divinity itself.

He dipped it into the juice within the Bowl of Vitrumesh and poured some of the contents into a glass pitcher that I recognised, perhaps the only surviving work from the shop. I glanced at Marcella to see if she showed signs of recognising it too; the last I had seen of its translucent red Celtic knotwork was when she had admired it in the shop before we had... well, you know.

Her face gave no signs.

Amatus approached Memor.

"Drink."

Memor looked at me.

"Beer?"

"The Juice of Vitrumesh," I explained. "It is drunk in homage to the eastern origins of Vitrumesh, and the citrus and pomegranate orchards on the banks of the Euphrates."

"So, not beer?"

"Beer will come later. First, we honour his origins. Later, we honour what he gave us."

Memor looked disappointed, but presumably not, as I would have been, from having to wait for beer. He was disappointed by the prospect of drinking it later on. After a moment, he took the jug from Amatus' hands and raised it to his lips. Its long tapered neck made for uneasy drinking.

"The... difficulty of the vessel signifies the pains with which Vitrumesh relinquishes his secrets," I said.

His eyes darted to mine as he hefted the vessel upwards, allowing a small portion of juice to dribble down his throat.

"More," said Amatus as Memor lowered the jug. Amatus watched him with an unblinking gaze as Memor raised the jug again. Redness spilled down the side of his mouth and stained the pristine white of his toga. "Still more."

When Amatus finally did allow him to lower the jug, Memor must have consumed three times his daily intake of fruit.

Marcella reached for the jug to have her share.

"No. Not you." Amatus was adamant.

Now her eyes shot to mine.

"Ah... Vitrumesh..." Thinking up excuses on the fly was hard. How in Hades did politicians do it so liberally?

"Vitrumesh is a warrior-god. His sacred juice is to imbue strength in those men who would protect the home, rather than those weaker women who would be the home makers."

Admittedly, that's also what happens when politicians are left to think on their feet, without their script-writers. And it was a good thing for them that women had no say in their continued tenure in office. I would have noticed the reception my comment had received had I not been reaching for the jug to take a swig of my own. I prised it from Amatus' fingers and held it to my lips.

The trickle I received tasted sweet, before I felt Amatus' hand pulling the jug downwards.

"Floral, with acidic notes. A hint of citrus," I commented as I kept the jug from Amatus' grasp and passed it around the remaining congregation. I returned to the altar and addressed Vitrumesh directly, picking up where I had left off.

"Oh, extraordinary Vitrumesh, we heed the tales of your splendour. We consider the sacrifices you made for us in defeating the great serpent Oomes. The great serpent, who would take what was not his, who would slither into places unwelcome to him and whisper, and repeat, and concoct. Of your battle, a battle that could not be won on land or water or in fire. Of the injuries you sustained until you combined the might of all three - the produce of the land, the water of the river, the fire of the stove, and drowned the lecherous being in a river of beer.

Right on cue, the Tarraconensis Troupe picked up their chant again, raising in volume and octave for dramatic effect.

"Oh, potent Vitrumesh, we sacrifice to you today—"

Don't worry. All rams, pigs and bulls within the immediate area were safe from becoming Vitrumesh's evening meal. Instead, we sacrificed something else near and dear to his heart, and mine. Amatus brought it forth and passed it into my hands, within the sacred table-top sized Amphora of Vitrumesh.

"—this beer, brewed in the hearth of the home you would protect. A beer with deep character and chewiness, meaty and hearty, a taste that lingers on the palette."

This, despite the description, was not a sample of Tiber's finest. In fact, it was not a sample of Tiber's at all.

"You're not pouring any of my beer out all over the floor. Use your own," had been Tiber's response to my request.

"I don't have any left, Augustalis smashed it all."

"Then that's your problem, not mine. Go find someone else's."

But Varro had a better idea; rather than spend more money, he hunted around outside for any old mulch and leaf mold, mixed it with water and boiled it down on the stove to make a dark brew that would pass well enough as the barbarian's favourite booze to fool Memor's epicurean senses. Tiber approved of our methods but he had not checked with his wife before we had made use of her pots and pans. Tiber had almost joined me on the floor with a blanket that night.

But now, I turned to face my congregation, amphora in hand. Memor's expression fell a little as my eyes rested upon him and I lingered, enjoying his discomfort at the thought he might have to taste the liquid.

The moment dragged; Memor's face dissolved into a wince

and he tried not to make a show of rubbing his tummy before I up-ended the vessel and poured out the entire contents on the floor.

It smelt of wet dog as it pooled and splashed and seeped between the floorboards but, to be fair, the aroma was not entirely out of place.

"You sacrifice all of it?" Memor sounded relieved.

"Vitrumesh is quite a heavy drinker."

I passed the empty vessel to Amatus and addressed Vitrumesh once more.

"Oh magnificent Vitrumesh," I intoned. "We beseech you today to provide your help, to lead us on the path to reunite Lucius Marcius Memor and his niece Marcella, with their niece and cousin, Vilbia, to whom they provide great love and respect. We ask you to protect them as you would protect any family from the betrayal of Oomes. We approach you with truth in our heart and honesty upon our lips."

That ought to get his heart beating a little faster I thought, as I stole a glance at him. It was working; he did look to be breathing a little heavier, trying to suppress a cough as the rosemary aroma tickled his throat.

I reached out towards Amatus and he brought over the augur's staff. He came to stand between me and the others, so that they would not see his face as he passed it into my hands.

"Slow it down," he hissed.

"What?"

"Slow... it... down," he said under his breath as he moved away. "We need more time."

I was taken aback. Seven words was the longest communication I had heard from Amatus. Time for what? I looked at the gathered. They stared back at me. I glanced down at the draining beer water and was hit by inspiration.

That inspiration came from Varro-with-the-gimpy-leg, of all

people, and the play, Electra. I just needed to sound confident in my observations.

"The beer..." I said, waving my arm to draw their attention to it. "Look how it drains."

"So?"

"Vitrumesh has requested that we meditate upon our desires and consider what we would request of him."

Memor was not amused. "What?"

"The beer drains away from the river" – of course it would, the floorboards were warped in that direction – "which means that Vitrumesh is not yet ready to hear us, he wants us to dwell upon our request longer. To be certain it is what we want."

"For how long?"

"Until he gives us the next sign."

I took great pleasure in making everyone stand for the duration of the Reflective Period of Vitrumesh. The actors were well accustomed to the physical demands of spending extended periods of time on their feet. Marcella had youth on her side. Memor did not.

It was hard to feel sorry for him.

We gave them a good twenty minutes to mull over what they had done. I mulled over what I had done in my life to get to this point, but I decided that was a bad idea by the time I reached "when I turned three, I glued three sheets of papyrus to my face and told everyone I was an elephant."

Enough was enough. It was time for that next sign.

"Oh look," I pointed to the puddle. "The beer no longer drains away. The pool that remains has stilled. That means that Vitrumesh is now ready to be still, listen, heed our words and advise us."

I raised the augur's staff and mimicked the priests I had seen as best as I could, drawing a rectangle in the air - the 'frame' within which we would be watching for Vitrumesh's sign.

Anything outside of that frame did not count. Anything inside was a divine message.

The frame I drew delineated the space around the back door of the building, ready for Draco to enter and put the fear of Vitrumesh into us all.

"I don't see anything," grumbled Memor.

"Haruspex, you of all people should know that these things take time."

"Oh, for Minerva's sake!"

Draco's handlers had been instructed to wait a few minutes after the start of the augury before releasing him into our midst. I returned my gaze to our frame and blinked. The warm light cast by the lanterns seemed to be greying and hurt my eyes despite no change in their strength.

We waited for the sign until Marcella's voice cried out, "There!"

Vitrumesh had sent his sign. It was not the sign I was expecting.

Vilbia herself now stood in the doorway, smack bang in the middle of my augury square.

***

Marcella was moving fast.

"It's her!"

"No, wait—" I caught her arm as she passed and pulled her towards me.

"Grab her!" Memor took three steps before collapsing to one knee with a grunt. "Stop her! Marcella—"

For an instant, I thought Memor wanted to err on the side of caution, to stop Marcella from racing after her cousin, but one glance at his face told me otherwise. It was so full of hatred and rage and frustration. "That girl is ours! Bring her to me! Augustalis!"

Oh shit.

"Run!" I shouted to Vilbia, who stood wide-eyed and frozen in the doorway. With a squeal, she turned and darted into the dark, but in which direction I didn't see as in that moment I felt pain like you wouldn't believe.

Having elbowed me in the throat and brought her knee into that part of the body upon which the Romans model their little winged good-luck symbols, Marcella slipped from my grasp and bolted after her cousin, leaving me crumpled on the floor next to Memor.

"Varro..." I tried to shout but it came out more as a wheezed aspiration than a hearty roar.

The Tarraconensis Troupe decided enough was enough. The bad reviews from this performance were something that they did not need and they scarpered, our witnesses all scattering off through the delivery doors and into the night, leaving myself, Memor and Amatus to ourselves.

Amatus was no help at all.

He stood with his back against a wall and watched from the shadows of his hood as if the whole farce was a performance put on for his sole benefit.

"No—" came Vilbia's voice from beyond the doorway and I looked back to see the form of Augustalis filling the frame. He threw Vilbia into the room and she landed nearby and crawled towards me. I tried to shelter her behind me but realistically there was not much I could do - Augustalis was three times the man I was, and I mean that in the physical sense, not the metaphorical one.

"I'm sorry, I just had to see... to see him humiliated," she whimpered as Marcella returned and helped Memor to his feet. Once his balance returned, he yanked his arm free from her grasp and rubbed his belly with a wince.

"Well, priest," he said, his voice hoarse. "It seems your

Vitrumesh came through for us after all."

"Leave her alone."

Memor raised an eyebrow.

"You seem surprised. Did you really think your pathetic little Parthian godling could really hold sway over Minerva?"

"You don't speak for Sulis," Vilbia spat. "You never did."

Memor chuckled, a chuckle that turned into a cough. "You should hold your tongue, girl," he said when he could draw breath. "Augustalis…"

Augustalis stepped towards us, a length of rope held taut between his hands. I struggled to get to my feet. It wasn't easy, but a girl's future was at stake and some would say that was more important than the crippling pain I bore now.

"What—"

"I'm sorry, Titus," Memor said in a tone that implied he was anything but. "But we all knew where this was heading."

"And where was that?"

He was torn between deciding whether or not I was vying for time or genuinely asking. I wish that it had been the former but he assumed correctly that it was the latter.

"If it's any consolation," he said, "I'm told Vitrumesh is a god of water and fire - he'll probably keep an eye on you as we dump you in the river and burn this place to the ground…woah."

That was a long sentence for someone who gets short of breath easily in the rosemary-heavy air. He was blinking hard and almost gulping in breath, but still he waved Augustalis forward. Augustalis smirked. I don't know what I had ever done to offend him, but he appeared keen to take his revenge regardless. He looped the rope once more around his hands for a better grip; a garrotte to finish what the spoon had started.

My vision greyed as time slowed and I felt Vilbia move around me to stand between us. I couldn't die here. I was too far away from Rome for Father to put his fire-starters to good use, and I never ended up getting that funeral mask made.

"Yeah, go on Augustalis, kill him," Vilbia goaded, "and then we'll all have a nice little chat about what you've been up to for the last couple of years."

"Wait—" Marcella grabbed at Augustalis who tried to shake her off.

"It's been him all along, Marcella," said Vilbia. "Hiding me. Not Calvus. Augustalis."

"What is she talking about?" Marcella asked.

"Oh, for Minerva's sake," swore Augustalis. "Don't listen to her!"

Then, Marcella did something that I have to begrudgingly respect her for. She slapped Augustalis hard across his face. I think it hurt her more than it hurt him, but the surprise stopped him in his tracks.

"What does she mean?" she demanded.

"Calvus wants to hand me over," Vilbia continued, trying to protect me by deflecting their attention. "Augustalis has been keeping me safe—"

"I knew it!" Marcella spun to face Memor and threw her arm towards Augustalis. "I knew it, I tried to warn you—"

"Augustalis has been fooling them, Marcella!" Memor said, waving her to silence. "He's already explained this. He found them days ago, he's been trying to coerce them out, to come quietly until this blundering idiot—"

"Days ago?" shouted Vilbia. "Years! He's been hiding me from you for years, he betrayed you, he helped me escape—"

"You ungrateful—" Memor stepped towards us but doubled over, clutching his belly. "Wicked child, the lies..." He grimaced. "I need to sit... Marcella..."

There were no chairs; I had taken great pride in that rather stoic feature of Vitrumesh's ceremony. Marcella hurried to him and supported his weight as best she could. I was aware that this then left Augustalis unencumbered, but he was too busy gawping at Memor to take advantage of his release.

"You ungrateful..." he repeated.

"Ungrateful?" Vilbia was astounded. "Ungrateful? What was there to be grateful for? Marcella was the one you loved. She was the one with the toys. She was the one the nursemaids doted on. She was the one with the power to get rid of them if they showed any inclination to help me too. Jovina was the only person who ever even tried! I grew up knowing that I was to be the price for Marcella's happiness. I was a slave in all but name!"

"You served a purpose!" Memor found the strength to roar. "How could you ever be anything different? Daughter of an actress? A father who was a carouser? And yet how they lived, while Marcia and I... They should have died sooner, but I needed them!"

He blinked hard, several times.

"You killed them?" Vilbia's voice was quiet, and yet we all heard her words clearly.

"It was my pleasure to. Five years! Five years of them listening to my every word, believing that I had healed her, had healed you. I was just careful with the dose. But they had served their purpose too, I didn't need them. I didn't need any of them any m—"

He fell to the floor as Marcella released him, her eyes wide, her face ashen.

"You... you killed them all? You killed my parents too?"

He stretched an arm towards her, gulping air. "No, no - your mother... she did not eat enough, it was a ruse... it should not have... she... she... oh, Marcia."

"And my father?"

"You didn't need him. You had me. You were meant to have your mother... augh!" He was curling more into a ball as he spoke. "What... what have you done to me?"

The inhuman shriek that followed did not come from Memor.

It came from Amatus. He threw back his hood and danced around the room like a madman, laughing and hooting.

"See!" he screamed. "See! What's good for the goose is good for the gander! See!" He pointed a finger in Memor's face, but I don't think Memor could see him any more. "You! You did this! You did this and now look at you!"

In the confusion, I grabbed Vilbia and thrust her towards the front door.

"Go," I hissed.

"But—"

"Go! I'll be fine."

She glanced at Memor and Amatus, both oblivious to the rest of us, then back at me and nodded before she legged it towards the door.

But Augustalis noticed her go and as I moved between them, I ended up on the ground for the second time as he was off and after her. Marcella shrieked and I looked back.

Memor was no longer curled up. His entire form was rigid, convulsing on the floor as Amatus continued to dance around him. Both had their arms raised in a macabre imitation of each other - Memor with locked elbows as he jerked and twitched; Amatus in a more fluid motion as he spun in a circle, laughing at the ceiling.

With a final "yah-ha-ha-ha!", he sprinted out of the back door.

"No you don't!" Marcella took off after him.

"Marcella—" I shouted after her, and twisted my head to look to the front door. "Vilbia..."

Memor's convulsions were subsiding, his lips blue and his breath was shallow.

I made my decision.

Hauling myself up, I sprinted to the front door and burst through it—

—ending up, once again, flat on my face in the dirt.

"What?" I had tripped over the prostrate form of Augustalis. If a pool of blood and a vacant stare reflecting the moonlight can tell you anything, they can tell you that Augustalis was very definitely dead.

23

"Gah!" I scooted away and almost bowled Varro-with-the-gimpy-leg over as well. I stared up at his face - it was the epitome of ecstatic.

"Well, that was fun!" he beamed.

"Fun? Fun?"

Taking in more of the scene around me, I realised that Varro was holding Vilbia's hand, keeping her behind him. In his other hand, he held a rusty old short-sword, a gladius of the legions. With no hands free, he awkwardly wiped the flat of the blade against his thigh, rubbing off some of the blood onto his cloak.

"Be a dear," he said to Vilbia, "and find my stick, would you?"

She stared at him open mouthed. We both did, until she said, "um, of course," and moved away to hunt.

"Scare them, Varro!" I shouted at him. "We were meant to scare them!"

He shrugged. "This way's better."

"Oh, gods!"

I heard a noise from inside. I both hoped and feared that it would be Memor regaining consciousness, but at this point it would not have surprised me had it been Memor's shade, already arisen and seeking the help of the Harpies to haunt me for the rest of my days; the human-vulture hybrids flocking to drag me off to Tartarus to endure divine punishment for all that had transpired within the last few moments.

"Give me that," I held out my hand for the sword.

"Do you know how to use it?"

"Just give it here" – I snatched it from his grasp as Vilbia brought forth his crutch – "before you do any more damage with it. What am I meant to tell Tiber?"

"Tell him it went well."

I glared at him, then sidled around Augustalis and back inside. Memor was as I left him, unmoving and distinctly the wrong colour. I could not even be certain if his chest rose any more with his breathing.

The Altar of Vitrumesh remained behind him, the Bowl of Vitrumesh in pride of place at the centre. The bottom of the bowl was in shadow, marking the vague and considerably-reduced level of the juice within. My stomach made a 'gallooping' sound at the sight of it - just what effects of its poison lay in store for me now?

And behind the altar, stood Marcella. She was alone. Her expression was... well, flat is the only word to describe it. She did not look upset, she did not look happy, she just... looked.

"You said you would make me glass of all the colours of the rainbow." She raised her eyes from the bowl to me in the door frame. "Are you going to kill me too?"

I looked down at the bloody sword, held limply between my fingers. I tossed it into a corner.

"Marcella—"

"You know, I suppose I should thank you. All those years. All those missed years with my parents."

She moved around the altar and squatted next to Memor. Not too close, but not too far, as she regarded his face with no change in her expressionless face.

"I should be..." a moment of confusion flickered in her eyes but it did not last. "I should be sad, or scared, or... I don't know. I should be something. Why am I not something?"

In time, the shock would wear off, and I did not want to be there when it happened. She reached over and fussed with his thinning hair.

"What happens now?" she asked.

I released a pent-up breath.

"Now, you go home."

"Home?"

"To your mansion half the size of Minerva's temple. The one that takes five wrong turns and six unhelpful guides to find. To your statue of Doris, and your fiancé."

She stood, drawing herself up to look at me, pure, hot hatred appearing on her face.

"You think this is over?"

"I know it is. Because I know that you have a small birthmark on your pelvis."

"I don't follow."

"Marcella..." I didn't want to spell it out, but I had to. "You are the most eligible bride in Aquae Sulis. You are independently wealthy - all that was your father's is now yours, all that was Memor's is now yours, and I daresay that is much more than he puts on show. But... you're not a virgin, Marcella. That was to be enough for Memor to justify thrusting Vilbia into slavery, the girl he saved who betrayed them all. What would that blight on your reputation do to you, Marcella?"

Oh, the death-look she gave me.

"And how do you suppose you'll get away with the murder of the most powerful man in Aquae Sulis? People will notice he's gone."

I glanced down at Memor's form, and across at the bloody sword in the corner.

"Tell them you were set upon by bandits on the way home."

She stared at me in silence for a moment.

"All that was his is now yours. It was always meant to be yours in the first place, until he challenged that will..." I reminded her.

"Fine."

There was no love lost between her and her uncle now. She spun on her heal to leave.

"Why, Marcella?" I asked to her retreating back. She glanced over her shoulder at me. "Why would you go along with his plans for your cousin?"

"It was my right. My life. It was going to be perfect. But she was always there, in the corner. The reminder of Uncle Gaius' shame, the blight on my family's reputation of treating her like an equal, a woman like..." Her eyes met mine and she stopped talking.

"I loved you," I said.

"And that's your problem, not mine."

You know what? I'm the man with the dubious honour of owning the last house on a track into a swamp, a two-room abode built on the place within which the most water accumulates after rain before draining down to the creek.

And yet I had never felt so dirty in my life.

24

Titus Laelius Calvus to his dear, but frustrating, sister, Laelia Tertia.

Greetings!

I know you've given me up for dead, but you can cut the celebrations now, because I most certainly am not.

Disappointing, I know.

I hope the wine was Falernian, grown at least within sight of Mons Massicus, if not from halfway up its slope.

You may wonder at the couriers that I have sent to deliver this message. Allow me to introduce you. Jovina is the most annoying person you will ever meet, her twin babes enjoy chomping on rocks and gravel in graveyards, and never, ever, ask her about her garden shed. Vilbia also answers to Pacatus, but she prefers Vilbia and she will not, under any circumstances, dig barley trenches for you.

But they are good people, and I hope that you can use your newly-acquired status as the wife of the brother of the assistant of the Prefect who advises the Emperor Hadrian himself, to find them a stable house (stable, as in not likely to fall down, not stable as in filled with straw) and a reliable income. But not as a cleaner. I would not wish Jovina's cleaning skills upon my worst enemy.

They bring with them a wedding present from me to you. Look after it well - it is a deep bowl, more colourful and mysterious than any I have ever seen and, unfortunately, not a creation of my own skilled hands however I did play a significant role in causing it to be made. Jovina will explain, but let me assure you that it has been thoroughly washed and will serve you well.

On the subject of income, I regret to advise that it may be some time before I can join you in Rome once again. Never fret,

I am well settled here and happy. But, you can tell Father that the money that remained from his strongbox was spent on courier fees, getting these two ladies and their baggage (babies and otherwise) to you all the way from Britannia. But don't tell him the Britannia part. And, don't tell him the conditions within which they may have needed to travel. I had intended to voyage in comfort back to you should the need arise, but that budget probably did not stretch too far when divided into four tickets.

With that in mind, could you also give them a comfortable bed to sleep in until such time as a stable house is found? I think they've earned it.

I would ask you to pause reading this letter now and allow Jovina to tell you of the circumstances in which she has travelled to your doorstep. It is quite a lengthy tale, so I advise sitting down with some lunch.

Have you done it?

Good.

Now, here are the things Jovina probably didn't tell you.

1) I now have five years of contractual purchases to make from Dio before I can afford to travel home. The payment we made of Jovina's house for his help in staging the Ceremony of Vitrumesh didn't stretch to the disposal of two bodies, but, I tell you what, I have never been so relieved as when I signed away exclusive rights as the sole supplier for our workshop, in return for him bringing his dinghy, Fish Killer, up to the Dock of Vitrumesh and rowing those two away to I don't know where (and hopefully never will).

2) I had no idea how to convince Tiber to stay on in order to meet those contractual obligations but, at the time, that was future Calvus' problem.

3) I have solid circumstantial evidence that this whole fiasco could have been averted had Dio just been a little more forthright in his information - along with supplying Petronax with the natron for the mummification, it turns out he also supplied the decoy body for the funeral. He mentioned this in passing to me as if it was the most normal thing in the world, with a "what? It was just some slave I picked up cheap from the quarry. Don't give me that look, he was already dead."

4) Dio scares me.

5) So does Amatus. We don't know where he went, but Varro finally told us who he was. Get Jovina to repeat the bit of the story where I passed a boy selling foraged berries as a cheap snack on the streets of Aquae Sulis, then jump ahead a little to the meeting with Memor. Did she tell you about the interruption to our conversation that we bore with grace, as Memor provided instructions to Amatus about how to deal with his annoying neighbour, Zoticus? Those instructions resulted in much more than just giving Zoticus the squits as intended (and I can tell you, having sampled a small amount of the Juice of Vitrumesh myself, those squits are not pleasant. Also, I hear that the Tarraconensis Troupe subsequently cancelled three performances for undisclosed reasons). Zoticus had a similar constitution to Memor, and, well... those who live by the suspiciously cheerful little red berries die by the suspiciously cheerful little red berries.

6) I am undecided as to whether I should turn to investigative work as a side income. You never know. It could be fun. The multiple near-death experiences were probably something I could do without, and it's made everyone I care about here angry with me, but... well... I am quite chuffed with the way it turned out to be honest, as there are now two good people safe and sound after a lifetime of threats and disaster. But I don't know what to call myself. My favourite is still 'Laelius Calvus: the nude investigator'. Tiber has suggested 'Laelius Calvus: the bloody idiot', Nux prefers 'Laelius Calvus: the incompetent one' and Jovina would probably go with 'Laelius Calvus: the gods-cursed son of a harpy'. But perhaps I should just go with the least judgemental suggestion, made by Enica - 'Laelius Calvus: the well-meaning investigator.' That might be the only one to ever win me an actual paying customer.

Please write with your suggestions.

7) We interred Eratosthenes as best we could in his tomb. We partook in one last act of blackmail to entice Petronax into

paying the final bill to the quarry so that we could take ownership of the room. Jovina and Vilbia took what few portable possessions they wanted from their house, Varro and I helped ourselves to some of the remaining furniture, and the rest we piled into the tomb so that Eratosthenes will have somewhere to sit as he enjoys the life eternal. The life eternal, in a waterlogged clay pit that turns everything inside damp. I wished him well as I departed the room and left him behind. I hope his ushabti servants have brought their own mops.

8) I've also inherited two chickens. I am undecided as yet if I will be having scrambled eggs or chicken stew for my dinner tonight. I'll allow Coquam and Pluma the chance to plead their case when I get home.

9) On the subject of seats, the Lounge of Uncertainty has been patched up. It seemed Varro picked up a few carpentry skills back in his days in the legions. And he's whittling himself his own beer-brewing spoon as he seems intent on helping me replenish my stock. I'm not entirely sure I'll ever be rid of Varro-with-the-gimpy-leg. But I will not be taking religious instruction from him again.

10) Maybe I have started my own religion. I never explained to Marcella that Vitrumesh was fake (though she probably worked it out, if we're honest). She carried the Mark of Vitrumesh away with her, which one day her children will ask her about. And their children will ask, and so forth down the line until in a thousand years, who knows? The great serpent Oomes may disappear with those few of us who invented the story, but perhaps Vitrumesh will grow to be a protector god, and a brutal one at that, who means business any time a charlatan travels halfway across the Empire to move in with a faithful family like some sort of weird creepy uncle, until such time as he becomes an actual weird creepy uncle, murders most of them and lives the high life on the threat of future enslavement. It's a very specific responsibility for a god, but I'm sure there's worse out there. We come from a culture that fashions little silver good-luck symbols in the shape of winged phalluses, after all.

*So, hang on to this new bowl of yours, it will protect you in
future should any of these events ever take place in your life.*
Your loving brother and father of a future god,
Titus.

***

As I finished drafting the letter, I looked across the table at
Tiber.
"Will you stay?" I asked him.
He said nothing but poured me a beer.

Author's Note

https://romaninscriptionsofbritain.org/
inscriptions/154

The curse placed upon the thief of Vilbia is an actual curse that was thrown into the waters of the Sacred Spring in Aquae Sulis, at an unknown date during the Roman era. By the time it was found in 1880, it had made its way through the plumbing to rest within the reservoir under what is today called the King's Bath – the large, iconic swimming pool within which Calvus enjoyed a pleasant, if possibly urine-tinged, soak with Varro-with-the-gimpy-leg.

Very little is known about Vilbia or those others listed within the curse. It is commonly thought that Vilbia was a girl who had been taken, but theories also exist that Vilbia may just be the nickname that somebody gave their particularly nice towel, or a misspelling of the word 'fibula', meaning 'brooch'. If Vilbia was in fact human, this curse is the only curse found at Bath to date that relates to actual bodily harm. All other translated curses refer to the theft of objects. However, the theft of a towel makes for a much less interesting mystery than the theft of a girl, and so the flight of Jovina and Vilbia from Memor took shape.

While devising Vilbia's background, I came across the name 'Lucius Vilbius Marcellus' within an inscription found in southern France, and so that man became Vilbia's fictional uncle, with his hypothetical daughter, Marcella, becoming her cousin. In an earlier draft of this book, Marcellus was written in as a character until I realised that his rather vague role could easily be taken up by Marcella herself and so poor old Marcellus joined the list of Vilbia's figurative victims from the spread of her 'illness'. The character of Marcellus is much more fondly remembered by his daughter than the character I had written; that version of Marcellus was an easily deceived religious fanatic with a chip on his shoulder and very little spine when it came to standing up to Memor.

Avid Roman historians may recognise the name Lucius Marcius Memor as the haruspex who constructed the altar within the temple courtyard at Aquae Sulis. Again, little is known about the historical Memor other than his name and that he hailed from northern Italy, but in the 1970s he featured as a character in the Cambridge Latin Course, a series of books still used to teach Latin. All other characters and events within this book are entirely fictional.

However, Calvus interacted with far more historically factual locations than he did with historically factual people. The only setting in this novel that has substantially survived and can be visited today is, of course, the Roman Baths at Bath – once the baths and Temple of Sulis Minerva at Aquae Sulis. The most famous image of those baths today – that of the King's Bath mentioned above, is largely a Victorian-era reconstruction and no longer situated under a massive Roman vaulted ceiling, but that particular feature is less than a quarter of the surviving archaeological remains that can be visited and explored.

Within Londinium, Calvus and Tiber's workshop is at the location of an archaeological site at modern-day Bishop's Court, within which furnaces and glass-blowing waste were found. When in use, the furnaces would have overlooked the Fleet River and a nearby watermill. The workshop is thought to have been built at about the time in which this novel is set, and the good news for Tiber and Calvus is that it might have been larger than described in this novel, so there's room for their enterprise to expand in future.

Tiber lives near to modern-day 1 Poultry Place, a large office complex within the City of London. Construction of the building in 1997 unearthed a relatively industrial area of Londinium, hence Tiber's next-door neighbour being a carpenter, and his threat to join the other glass-blowing workshops known to have existed just east of the fort.

The fort, amphitheatre, forum, basilica, and the 'governor's palace' (a large complex perhaps associated with the province's Proconsul) are all well-known and confirmed features of Londinium at this time, although the true nature of the 'governor's palace' is open for debate. Dio's buildings are within an area known to have housed plenty of warehouses on the northern bank of the Tamesis, near the city docks.

Heading south across the bridge to modern-day Southwark (the bridge being very close to where the modern London Bridge is today), Memor and Marcella stayed at a building believed to be an elegant mansio currently being excavated prior to the construction of the Liberty of Southwark complex. As I was drafting this novel, the incredibly-well preserved dining room mosaic was discovered with perfect timing and it is the largest mosaic found in London for more than 50 years. Calvus mentions that it was in the shadow of the Procurator's residence, for which I have appropriated the large urban villa known to have existed at Winchester Palace. This potential connection with the Procurator has been suggested by archaeologists such as Dominic Perring, and it makes a lovely image of the Proconsul on the north bank of the Thames, and the Procurator on the south bank of the Thames, glaring at each other across the water each time they clashed in their respective political roles!

The Temple of Mars Camulus and the Imperial Cult is an actual temple complex located at modern-day Tabard Square but I have brought its construction forward forty-odd years because it was too perfect a setting for the novel to let a little thing like 'it hadn't been built yet' get in the way of using it. To compensate, the complex described in the story is smaller than the factual site, with only one of the two known temple buildings having yet been constructed. It is believed to have been built around or after 160 AD.

The plaque quoted in the story and dedicated by Tiberinius Celerianus was found during excavations. It is the earliest reference yet found to the term 'Londoners' (albeit in Latin). It also refers to the 'divinities of the Emperors', which is taken to be a reference to Marcus Aurelius and his co-ruler Lucius Verus (or, after Verus' death, Aurelius' son, Commodus), which is the first time Rome had been jointly ruled by two Emperors. As Marcus Aurelius was less than six months old when this novel is set, I reinterpreted this line to mean that the temple was jointly consecrated to Mars Camulus and the Imperial Cult, recognising the tendency for previous Roman Emperors to be declared gods upon their death. But it is highly unlikely that the temple actually had a meat cellar for storing carcasses for spit-roasts, or a place from which to spring large Central African rock pythons!

Acknowledgements

Move Over, Minerva would not have been possible without a large number of people who gave their time willingly and often freely to help, both directly and indirectly.

Without a team of family and friends to read, comment upon, edit and polish the early manuscripts, I doubt this novel would ever have been finished. I am grateful for the editing prowess of Jennifer Berkeley, Sybil Orr and Faye Bolton, and the early readers who were happy to check that the story was entertaining and made sense: Janet Lindsey-Noakes, Katie Martin and Keryn Rose, followed by the experienced, professional eyes of Fiverr freelancers Alice Creswell (@aliceiza) and Micheala Stahl (@micheala94).

To ensure that the historical detail of this book was as accurate as possible, I leaned heavily on a mountain of factual research undertaken by others. While there are hundreds of books and websites from which I gleaned details both small and large, there are a number of resources that I have relied upon for their in-depth information prepared by dedicated volunteers and staff. I thoroughly recommend that anyone writing in the period should check out these troves of information, principally: Roman Inscriptions of Britain (romaninscriptionsofbritain. org), ORBIS: the Stanford Geospatial Network Model of the Roman World (https://orbis.stanford.edu/), Celtic Personal Names of Roman Britain (https://www.asnc.cam.ac.uk/ personalnames), and Perseus Digital Library (https://www. perseus.tufts.edu/hopper). I also thank anyone who has ever thought to make a website about some truly niche topics, such

as a History of Glassmaking in London (glassmaking-in-london.
co.uk), travel blogs that describe how the sacred springwater at
the Roman baths in Bath tastes, and horse care YouTube
channels that describe how to mount a horse that does not wish
to be mounted.

About the Author

Thea Allen grew up in Tamworth NSW, where she discovered that her growing love of ancient history and mysteries could be combined when her school librarian gifted her a copy of Lindsey Davis' *The Silver Pigs*, which still sits proudly on her bookshelf.

She has a Bachelor of Arts in history and archaeology and now lives near Lismore NSW with her young family. *Move Over, Minerva* is her first novel.

www.ingramcontent.com/pod-product-compliance
Lightning Source LLC
Chambersburg PA
CBHW010346220726
48290CB00016B/2654